CM00741575

SPECIAL MESSAGE TO READERS

THE ULVERSCROFT FOUNDATION
(registered UK charity number 264873)

was established in 1972 to provide funds for research, diagnosis and treatment of eye diseases. Examples of major projects funded by the Ulverscroft Foundation are:

- The Children's Eye Unit at Moorfields Eye Hospital, London
- The Ulverscroft Children's Eye Unit at Great Ormond Street Hospital for Sick Children
- Funding research into eye diseases and treatment at the Department of Ophthalmology, University of Leicester
- The Ulverscroft Vision Research Group, Institute of Child Health
- Twin operating theatres at the Western Ophthalmic Hospital, London
- The Chair of Ophthalmology at the Royal Australian College of Ophthalmologists

You can help further the work of the Foundation by making a donation or leaving a legacy. Every contribution is gratefully received. If you would like to help support the Foundation or require further information, please contact:

THE ULVERSCROFT FOUNDATION
The Green, Bradgate Road, Anstey
Leicester LE7 7FU, England
Tel: (0116) 236 4325
website: www.ulverscroft-foundation.org.uk

GOOSEBERRY FOOL

Willow's fields of gooseberries and strawberries are bursting with fruit and open for business. This heralds the start of a long hot summer, and the chance to reap the rewards of all her hard work. But Willow is not the only one with a project. Her husband Jude has plans of his own; and when she glimpses the future he is proposing for their land, she must come up with something to make him change his mind — and fast . . .

EMMA DAVIES

GOOSEBERRY FOOL

NOTTINGHAM COUNTY
COUNCIL

LINFORD
Leicester

First published in Great Britain in 2017

First Linford Edition published 2022
by arrangement with
Bookouture
London

*A catalogue record for this book is available
from the British Library.*

ISBN 978–1–4448–4799–4

Published by
Ulverscroft Limited
Anstey, Leicestershire

Printed and bound in Great Britain by
TJ Books Ltd., Padstow, Cornwall

This book is printed on acid-free paper

1

Jude Middleton was a very lucky man. He was also terrified of being poor. This fear, given to him by his father, and which had stalked him since his teenage years, now resonated through every part of his being as his powerful car whispered through the grimy streets and away from the city. How did people live like this? In dirty streets, and dirty houses, the cigarettes and booze they fed on the only things that got them through the day. These props were a necessity, he could see that, but they destroyed so much, used up too much of their meagre amount of money, and left nothing good behind, least of all hope.

It made him shudder to think about it, but the city was a necessary evil; from the over-air-conditioned and sterile offices, to the cheaply made clothes of the arrogant young go-getters he met with; from the smell of the traffic fumes

1

to the overpowering perfumes worn as part of a uniform. But whilst they were necessary, they were also forgettable, and Jude had been trained in the art of self-preservation for years. As the miles disappeared beneath his tyres, Jude shed their layers from his skin as a snake might. Within half an hour, it was all a distant memory.

* * *

The nights were beautifully light now and the scent from the stocks along the edge of the house rose up to greet him as he made his way up the path to his front door. A child's bicycle lay abandoned on the front lawn, ready to be picked up again tomorrow once school had ended for the day. The trailing white rose which burgeoned over the porch, had stems heavy in bloom, and their heads brushed his as he placed his key in the lock.

Willow was waiting for him in the hall-way, her eyes shiny at seeing him, just as they always were. She had on another of her wafty dresses (as Jude referred to them); it suited her, with her long, wavy blonde hair and slight figure, her bare feet covered by its trailing hem on the thick carpet. He dropped his bag by the door and gathered his wife into his arms, breathing in the smell of orange blossom which she always brought with her. She slipped her hand into his and led him towards the kitchen.

As always, the table and work surfaces were a jumble of school bags and books, toys, hair slides, and the general detritus of a busy day of childhood. It was the same every day, and Jude felt reassured by their presence. The girls were munching their way through fish finger sandwiches by the look of things; great doorsteps of homemade wholemeal bread, dripping with butter. His stomach rumbled at the thought of what Willow might have made for his own supper, the unsatisfactory steak he had eaten at lunchtime having done nothing to appease his appetite.

He stood in the doorway for a minute,

anticipating one of his favourite times of day, and sure enough a few seconds later Beth spied him, giving her customary squeal. In an instant, both girls had released themselves from the table and rushed to his side.

'Daddy!' they chorused.

He swooped each of them up in turn, swinging them sideways and planting a trail of kisses across their wriggling stomachs.

'Do you know I think you've got even more beautiful during the day? Now how can that have happened?' he asked, laughing.

Amy, the eldest by eleven and a half minutes and far more forthright than her sister, gave a giggle. 'Don't be silly, Daddy,' she declared. 'That's impossible.' She smiled up at him through her long fair lashes. They were both so like their mother.

Willow came and took his jacket from him, folding it over her arm as she collected a glass from the cupboard and placed it on the table.

'Come and sit down, and I'll pour you some wine. Did it all go as planned?'

Jude thought of the meeting earlier that day, a meeting that had gone well on the way to sealing probably the biggest deal of his life. He wasn't ready to share the details yet, though, not when so much was at stake. His freedom from Andrew would be the biggest prize, but also the hardest won, and he would need to tread carefully if he was ever to pull it off.

'Well, there are still one or two finer points to be agreed on, but I'd say, yes, it went very well.' He smiled at Willow, wondering what else she would expect him to say. He didn't want to lie, but perhaps under the circumstances . . . 'Andrew was very pleased at any rate,' he added, watching her face carefully. He knew she didn't have much time for her father-in-law, believing him materialistic and callous.

'Then that sounds like it could be the perfect end to the week, I'm so pleased.' She reached into the fridge and took out a bottle of chilled wine, pouring him a glass before leaning down and kissing the top of his head. 'Supper will be half an hour yet, if you want to grab a shower. You must feel horrible after a day in the city.'

Jude nodded, and glugged back a large swallow of wine. He grimaced. 'God, this is revolting,' he said, the vinegary taste hitting the back of his mouth. 'What is it?'

Willow turned back to the fridge and waved an airy hand. 'White wine, that's all I know.' She grinned. 'It was on offer.' She took out the bottle and handed it to him. 'Isn't it any good?'

Jude shook his head affectionately. 'One day,' he admonished her, 'I will get you to appreciate the finer points of wine's great beauty. Until then, please don't buy rubbish. We have a cellar full of the good stuff, so just choose one of them. We don't need to scrimp and save.' He took the bottle from her and stuck it back in the fridge.

He pulled Willow towards him and

kissed her, at first only intending for it to be a brief touch of the lips, but she smelled so good and his desire began to rise. It was only when there was a loud chorus of 'euww' from the girls that he pulled away, laughing.

'Isn't it time these rascals went to bed anyway?'

'We might not always be able to afford nice things,' Willow said.

Jude thought of the conversations that had ranged back and forth this afternoon. In a few weeks, his signature would be on the bottom of the papers that were being drawn up, and then . . . maybe she had a point, after all. The deal would secure him a good deal of money initially, but after that their life would most definitely have to change. He reminded himself that this was what he wanted, but old habits die hard, and he wasn't sure if he was ready for the sacrifice. But Willow must never see the doubt on his face, so he quickly shrugged it away. He flicked a playful finger against the end of her nose, and kissed it. 'What are we going to do with your mummy?' he said to the girls. 'Tell her to behave herself.'

Willow merely smiled, thinking of the little nest egg that her prudent house-keeping had saved her, and she turned back to the girls.

'Come on now scamps, daddy's right, it's time you were getting sorted. Finish your sandwiches, and then it's time for your bath. If you're quick, we'll have time for an extra couple of chapters of *Winnie the Witch*.'

Both girls looked imploringly at her, just as she knew they would. 'But no staying up tonight, mind. I know it's Friday, but it's our big day tomorrow, don't forget.'

'Strawberries!' shouted Beth. 'Yummy!' And she grabbed Amy's hand, practically dragging her from the table.

* * *

The light was finally leaving the day now, but the sky was still clear and wide. The first and brightest stars were beginning to

8

appear, and Willow hoped that tomorrow would stay fine. The forecast was good; like today, blue skies, but not too hot, and no rain, that was the main thing. She pulled the bedroom curtains closed and went to turn on the shower, the pale glow of the lamp beside her bed illuminating the curve of her skin as she walked.

She was aware that Jude had been watching her from the bed. He lay fully clothed; his city suit shed, and now relaxed in jeans and a T-shirt. She knew he'd join her in a few minutes, for what would be the perfect end to the day, and a languid smile passed over her face as she thought about soap sliding over skin. Willow inhaled the fragrant steam that billowed around her with the fresh scent of lemons and shivered in anticipation of his touch. She was already lost in the sensation when she felt Jude behind her, his naked body padding soundlessly into the wet room, and a small sigh escaped her as she felt his hand slip across her stomach and over one breast. She turned, moving her own hands.

★　★　★

It must have been towards three in the morning when she awoke. A slight shift in her consciousness that alerted her to the fact that Jude was no longer beside her. But even as she registered his absence from the bed, she knew that this was not the only reason for her wakefulness. Fleeting images came back at her, still veiled in a fug of sleep, yet unpleasant enough to wake her. She tried to grasp at them, but the wisps of memory disappeared. A moment later, she heard the toilet flush and as Jude returned to wrap his warm limbs around her back, she smiled to herself. There was much to do tomorrow, and finally, time to start putting into place the plans that she had begun to make a few weeks ago. Plans, in fact, that had come to her during another night of restless sleep plagued by strange dreams but plans which were so exciting that she now couldn't wait for the morning. As her thoughts drifted towards the recipes in grandma Gilly's notebook, she slept, the troubling images she had seen in her sleep all but forgotten.

2

It was her art teacher who once told Willow that no sky could ever be this blue. She hadn't believed him then, and today was confirmation of that. The colour was unbroken, stretching out into the cloudless sky until it reached the horizon, only then paling slightly. The air was soft — not harsh with the fierce heat of late summer, but a gentle pervasive warmth that made her skin smile.

The fields were ready, and in a few moments, Willow too would be all set. She just needed to post one more tweet and then she could do no more. But people would come, of that she was sure; they always did. She collected the bottles of water and snacks she had prepared and, snatching up her sun hat on the way out, she walked down the hallway. She paused for a moment by the back door, looking towards the room on her right as if weighing something up, and then with a glance at her watch, she pushed open the door.

Her grandma's old notebook was still on the table where she had left it yesterday, and she reached for it now, running her fingers across the cracked surface, its yellowed pages spilling out from the confines of the navy-blue cover. The little silver moon on the top right-hand corner of the cover flashed in the sunlight, and Willow smiled. She needed no further testament that her actions were the right ones. She closed the door behind her softly, and walked out of the house and down the path, her fingers brushing the tips of the lavender that grew there as she went. She skirted around the apple trees and made her way to the gate which stood in the corner of the garden. She smiled and took a deep breath, whispering a thank you to the sun. The strawberries were waiting.

Even this early in the morning, there were a few pickers around. They didn't officially open for another half an hour, but no one was ever turned away. The folks who came this early usually picked with a vengeance. They were not the spur-of-the-moment afternoon crowd looking for a punnet of delicious fruit to have with their tea, nor were they families revelling in a day in the sun. They had purpose these early birds; the whole day ahead of them, and by sundown, jar after jar would be filled with sweet sticky jam.

Jude had already opened the wide gates into the car park and set out the signs directing people where to go. He now stood beside their little wooden shop with his back to her, looking up the slight slope of the field, watching Amy and Beth ahead of him. They were in good hands, thought Willow. Peter, their student here for the summer doted on the girls and wouldn't let them out of his sight. Their enthusiasm for picking would wane in the weeks to come, but today, on their first day of opening, they were just as excited as she was.

She sidled up behind Jude, planting a kiss on the nape of his neck, the pale skin as yet uncoloured by the sun. All that would change soon, even though hats were a must, as was sunscreen, long days in the fresh air would soon bring a golden glow to them all.

'All set, Captain?' He grinned.

Willow smiled at his greeting. It was how he always addressed her here. Middleton Estates might own all this land, but Willow had never had anything to do with the day-to-day running of their company; that was Jude's domain. These fields, though, were hers to command.

'All set,' she replied, with a smile of her own.

'So where would you like me, Sir?' he asked, doffing an imaginary cap. 'I can pick, or I can man the barricades?'

Willow glanced at her watch. 'Actually, could you pick for me? I'd like to stay here for a bit, you know, to catch up with folk for a while.'

'Get the gossip more like,' argued Jude benignly. 'I know what you're like.' He motioned with his head towards the few women who were steadily picking fruit.

'Humour me,' she said. 'I don't get that many opportunities. Besides which, Freya is going to pop over in a bit. We've a few things to talk about.'

Jude narrowed his eyes. 'Oh ay. I heard they were having a bit of a change of direction at Appleyard. That wouldn't be what you're planning to discuss, would it?'

'It might be.' Willow grinned, laying a finger along the side of her nose. 'That and to see how things with Sam are working out.'

Jude rolled his eyes. 'Right, well, I'm definitely off then if it's going to be all soppy girl talk.' He picked up a stack of empty punnets from the table beside the shop doorway and threaded them up his arm. 'Enjoy your natter.' He plonked a kiss on her lips and set off up the field.

Willow watched him go, the soft linen of his summer 'uniform' sitting comfortably on his lithe body as he moved easily across the ground. God he was gorgeous.

★ ★ ★

At times, manning the barricades was a pretty apt description of Willow's morning as her customers jostled for room in the shop. But it was all good-natured, as people came to pay for their fruit or to collect punnets in readiness for picking. Many stayed to talk, light-hearted chatter with their neighbours, or with Willow herself, and a few, feeling weak-willed, succumbed to one of Willow's tempting cakes as well. And throughout it all, the summery smell of strawberries pervaded the air, pungent and sweet, with their heady invitation to be eaten, fingers and lips stained red with their juice. If Willow could bottle the smell and sell it, she'd do that too.

After a couple of hours, the initial swell of opening day visitors calmed and returned to the more usual steady movement, and suddenly there was Freya, grinning at Willow like a Cheshire cat.

'Oh, I haven't seen you in such a long time,' she cried. 'Much too long!'

'It has been,' agreed Freya. 'We mustn't ever let it get so long again. I don't even know how it happened.'

Willow stood back to get a better look at her friend, with her gleaming chestnut curls and wide green eyes. She wore an air of contentedness that brought a glow to her cheeks and a softness to her face. 'Life is good then,' she surmised.

'Oh, life is very good,' gushed Freya in reply. 'Very good indeed. Hard work, mind . . .'

'But since when has that ever stopped you?'

'I know . . . but it's different now somehow, you know?'

Willow giggled. 'Oh, I do know, Freya Sherbourne. It's coming off you in waves. Love. That's what it is, pure and simple.'

Freya blushed. 'Is it that obvious?' She grinned. She stood back to let a customer pass by. 'And what about you? You look great too, and busy by the look of things.'

'Oh, always,' she replied. 'And about to get busier if I have my way.'

'Which knowing you, you will.' Freya laughed. 'So, come on then, tell me what you're up to. I know you've got something up your sleeve, you sounded really mysterious on the phone.'

'Well, that rather depends on whether what I've heard is true . . . ' Willow trailed off, feeling a little guilty that she hadn't seen her friend for a couple of months and now here she was about to spring a proposition on her.

She was just about to continue when Jude appeared, carrying half a dozen more punnets full to the brim with strawberries. He took off his hat, and came over to kiss Freya.

'You look well,' he commented, catching Willow's eye. He stood back for a moment, looking between the two women. 'Oh, I'm sorry,' he directed at Freya, 'I don't think you two have met, have you? Can I introduce my wife, the slave driver?'

'Oh, ha bloody ha,' muttered Willow.

Freya giggled. 'Get on with you, Jude, you love it, you know you do . . . you might want to watch the staff, though, Willow, this chap seems to have eaten half your stock.'

It was true, Jude's shirt had a very obvious dribble of strawberry juice down the front.

Jude pulled a face. 'I'm a walking advertisement for the deliciousness of the crop, that's all.' He looked back at Freya. 'I don't even get paid . . . '

'My heart bleeds for you,' said Freya, miming playing the strings of a violin. 'Actually Jude, now that you're here, would you mind watching the shop for a minute? I just want to have a chat with Freya, you know, lovey dovey girly stuff, and I thought we could pop back to the house for half an hour or so . . . I'll bring some drinks out afterwards.'

Jude's smile was warm. 'Of course it's okay. Go on, I'll take over here.' He kissed Freya's cheek again. 'If I don't get to see you later, say hi to Sam for me. Tell him to give me a ring, it's about time we had a pint together.'

Freya nodded as Willow took her arm. She waited for a few moments until they were well clear of the shop before speaking again.

'What on earth was all that *wanting to talk about lovey dovey stuff* back there? That's not the impression you gave me on the phone.' She narrowed her eyes. 'What are you up to?'

They'd reached the garden gate now, and Freya paused while Willow fiddled with the catch. 'Only that I know it's a subject pretty much guaranteed to have the menfolk backing away in droves. I want to show you something, but strictly on the QT for now.'

'Okay . . .' said Freya slowly, following Willow up the path.

Once inside, Willow led the way back into the kitchen.

'Look, let's grab a drink and I'll explain.' She reached into the fridge and took out a glass jug decorated with daisies.

'Is elderflower okay?' she asked.

Freya nodded enthusiastically, looking rather pleased.

Once they each had a glass, Willow beckoned Freya back down the hallway, leading her into the room she had been musing in earlier. It was warm inside – a bit tired and musty, as though it had been shut up for too long. Apart from a sink, a long pine trestle table which held her grandmother's notebook, two chairs and a series of shelves running the length of one wall, it was completely empty.

Freya's eyebrows were raised. 'That's quite a transformation,' she said. 'When I last saw this room, it was full to the brim with coats, boots and toys. When did you do all this?'

'A couple of weeks ago. Three actually.'

Freya looked up, concern crossing her face. 'You gonna tell me why?' she asked softly, taking a seat at the table. Willow followed suit.

'I don't think I've ever actually shown you this,' she said, and pushed the notebook across the table towards Freya, where it sat looking suspiciously like a can of worms.

Freya stared at it.

'I'll explain. I know you all thought I

was weird when we were kids, especially Stephen —'

'Stephen thought everyone was weird . . .'

Willow smiled at the memory of Sam's brother. 'Yes, maybe. But we all joked about it, me included. I know my mum was different from everyone else's, but do you remember what she said just after you and Sam, well, you know, the Stephen thing.'

'You can say it you know, Willow. After I dumped Sam, ran off with his brother and then jilted him at the altar,' said Freya. 'I vaguely remember it. Your mum said everything would come right in the end and that I'd get Sam back again one day. But everybody told me that, Willow; they were just trying to make me feel better. No one was more surprised than me when it actually happened . . .' She looked down at the notebook and then back up at Willow. 'Actually, thinking about it, you weren't that surprised when I told you what happened at Christmas . . .'

23

Willow picked up the book and eased off the tie that was holding it closed. She took out an envelope tucked between the pages and held it out to Freya.

'Here it is in black and white,' she said. 'Mum sent me this letter at university, just after your wedding should have taken place. The first page is general chit chat and goings-on in the village etcetera, but you might want to read the second page.'

Freya took the letter, looking bemused. It was a long time ago, after all. She took out the thin white sheets and began to read.

... I saw Freya in the village shop only yesterday, and she looked awful, poor love. It was a brave thing to do, though; Jenny and Sarah were in there, clearly talking about her. They stopped of course when they saw her, but it was so obvious. I wanted to talk to her then to tell her that things would be okay, but by the time I'd paid for my things, she'd gone. She must have legged it pretty quick, and who can

blame her. Anyway, please tell her next time you see her, my dream was very explicit. It will take a long time, years even, but she was definitely with Sam, and it was definitely Christmas time, I could smell the pine from the tree like it was in the room with me. There was someone else there too, someone with black curly hair, but I couldn't see any more . . .

Freya looked up in shock.

'From what you told me that was pretty much how it happened, wasn't it?' asked Willow.

Freya nodded mutely. 'So Jessie knew,' she continued. 'She actually knew . . . '

Willow leaned over to touch Freya's hand. 'There were other things of course, things I never told you about back then; you all thought I was weird enough. I don't blame you for not believing me, but to me she was just my mum.'

'And just like her own mum I'm guessing?' Freya said, eyeing the notebook still in Willow's hands. 'So that's granny Gilly's, is it? Her book of spells.'

Willow looked at the ceiling. 'I know it sounds far-fetched, but you should see what's in here, Freya. Some amazing recipes apart from anything else, which is one of the reasons why I wanted to talk to you. But aside from that there are some . . . well, let's just call them remedies, shall we?'

Freya stayed silent for a moment, weighing up what she'd just been told. 'So why am I here?' she asked eventually.

Willow inhaled deeply, letting her breath out in a slow, controlled movement.

'Because I've had a few weird dreams of my own lately, nothing that momentous, but they've got me thinking about what we do here, or rather the potential for what we might do here. Once I started to think about it, I couldn't stop . . . only I might need your help.'

'Me?' asked Freya, surprised. 'What can I do?'

'Well, I heard on the grapevine that you and Sam are changing a few things at the orchard and that maybe you're not going to be making cider any more?'

Freya sighed. 'The jungle drums work well, don't they? My fault. When Sam and I got back together, I didn't realise quite how difficult it would be for him to up and leave the family business and his home. He's totally committed to Appleyard now, but still, having his brother as our main competitor down the road wasn't easy, and you know what Stephen's like.'

'Is he ever going to grow up, do you think?'

'Well, actually, it's early days, but I think there might be some progress in that direction. There's been something of a truce called lately, but I don't count my chickens where Stephen is concerned. I thought moving away from cider production and into juices instead might help Sam feel more settled, more like it was our business and not just mine any longer.'

Willow took a sip of her drink. 'And has it?' she asked, over the rim of her glass.

27

Freya's reply was immediate. 'Oh yes,' she said. 'Just try stopping us now; we've got that many plans. A range of our own juices for definite, perhaps other products too, and we're also going to set up a community juice pressing service so that locals or other small growers like ourselves can come and press their own fruit.'

Willow's grin was getting wider and wider by the minute.

'I take it that was what you wanted to hear.' Freya laughed.

'It might be . . . Do you remember the ice cream I made for Louisa and Phillip's ruby wedding anniversary? Well, that was one of granny's recipes, straight out of that notebook, and there are plenty more, all using the kind of soft fruits that I grow here. I thought I might try and have a go at making them again, properly I mean, to sell. What do you think? I could start with the gooseberry perhaps.'

Freya took another sip of her drink, holding the glass aloft and peering at the dew-coloured liquid. She squinted up at

Willow. 'I think you might need to borrow some of our elderflowers,' she said, amused. 'And what a totally brilliant idea!'

'Well, I'm not sure that 'borrow' is quite the right word, but if I could harvest your elderflowers, perhaps you might like to have some of the syrup I make back in return. You could use it for your own juices.'

'Serendipity!' Freya grinned. 'Although I really don't need anything in return, Willow. I didn't put the elderflowers there, Mother Nature did . . . but, now that you come to mention it . . . apple and elderflower . . . mmmm.'

'So do you think we might be able to come to some sort of an arrangement?' asked Willow.

Freya sat back in her chair. 'I'm certain we could. I'd want to run it by Sam of course, but it's just the sort of thing he'd love, I know it. God this is exciting.'

'That's what I thought,' nodded Willow. 'And it could be just the thing we need.'

Freya paused for a moment, her face falling a little.

'So I get why you've suddenly cleared this room out,' she said, obviously wondering how much to say. 'It would make a great workroom, but . . . ' She cocked her head on one side, watching Willow closely. ' . . . earlier on you said this was all on the quiet, as if you didn't want Jude to know about it. Is . . . is everything all right between you two?'

'Oh God yes, it's nothing like that. Well, it sort of is, but not in the way you mean.' She threw her hair back over her shoulder. 'Let's just say that I'm worried Jude is in danger of making some very bad decisions soon; business decisions, but ones that will affect our whole family. I'd like there to be an alternative, that's all, but I don't want to involve him until I'm sure it's something worth pursuing.'

Freya raised her eyebrows. 'Oh I get it, and then it will be his brilliant idea, right? That's the oldest trick in the book, Willow.' She smirked. 'You get exactly what you want, but Jude thinks it was his idea all along.'

Willow smiled in reply. 'Something like that,' she said.

'Well, I won't say a word, trust me. And I'll make sure that Sam keeps his mouth shut too. I should probably let you get back to your strawberries now, but why don't we meet up again one day in the week when Jude is at work, and then we can have a proper chat? There's someone else I think you should have a word with while we're about it. Someone who might also be able to help.'

'Anyone I know?'

'Oh yes, from way back, but let me have a chat to her first. If she's up for it, I might bring her along too.'

Willow rose from the table. 'Well, now I'm intrigued.'

'Good.' Freya winked. 'I'll give you a ring, shall I?'

3

Something wasn't right here. Willow shouldn't be able to feel the rain like this. Normally, when she stood by this gate, the canopy of trees overhead protected her from the worst of the elements. It wasn't until you reached the end of the wooded lane that the trees thinned out as the path sloped down towards to the clearing. Only then did you get a full view of the sky.

She shielded her face from the rain-drops that the wind was whipping into her eyes and looked up, raking the sky-line for any clue. Maybe she wasn't where she thought she was, but the sky was inky black, so there would be no help from the moon tonight. As she watched, an explosion of light struck out across the expanse of dark and she raised her shoulders, flinching in antic-ipation of the crashing noise that would surely follow as the lightning cracked open the night.

For a split second in the flare, the ground was illuminated before her, jagged scars cut through the fields, gouges through the pastoral landscape. Grasses, flowers, trees, all gone, just cracks of soil split wide, their muddy guts piled up in heaps. Willow could feel her feet oozing in the deep mud, rooting her to the spot, forcing her to look at the desecration in front of her.

She turned her head, another flash of lighting searing across her vision and this time row after row of houses stood, stretching out to the horizon, and above her head a huge wooden sign standing sentinel. She tried to pull her feet free from the soil, but as she struggled, sank ever deeper. The hairs pricked on the back of her neck, and panic rose in her throat . . .

Her breath came in heaving gasps as she woke, her nightdress heavy against her chest, sodden with her sweat, and it took her a few moments, eyes staring wildly out into the dark before Willow realised that she was safe, back in her room. She stretched out a hand to feel the smooth expanse of the sheets beneath her, the gentle cocoon of the pillow cradling her head. Beside her, Jude's rhythmic breathing stalled for a moment and she held her breath, but then it released once more in a sigh and with a faint snuffle, he resumed his peaceful sleep.

The clock beside the bed showed half past midnight; the dream had come quickly to Willow tonight, stronger than ever, and there was no longer any doubting its truth. She reached under her pillow and brought out the bundle of cloth which lay there, a small blue stone nestled within its folds. Even constrained within the soft muslin, its message had been a powerful one, and she was careful to keep the lapis lazuli from touching her skin; to do so right now would cause it to burn her like fire.

Very gently, she leaned across and slid open the drawer beside the bed, popping the bundle inside and, with a cautious glance at her husband, she lay back down and tried to calm both her mind and her breathing. Over the years there had been odd occasions when Willow had known without a shadow of doubt that things were going to happen, or she had seen things which had later come true. Intuition her mum had called it, being in tune with your feelings, and as a child Willow had been so used to her mum's eccentricities that she never thought anything of it. The things Willow had seen could be explained away, the feelings passed off as well-informed hunches. There had never been anything like the dreams she was having now. These were vivid, powerful even, and the truth was that they scared Willow a little; not only because of their intensity but because of the message they brought. She felt for Jude's fingers, feeling them close over hers as he slept. She looked at him fondly, but sadly.

Oh Jude, she sighed, *what have you done . . . ?*

* * *

Freya was met with a cloud of fragrant steam as Willow opened the door to the stillroom for her.

'Blinking heck, you don't hang around, do you?' she commented, breathing in the delicious fruity smell. She and Willow had sat in this room only a few days before but it was now no longer bare. Instead a new wooden work surface ran the length of one wall set with a huge cooker.

'That smells amazing,' Freya remarked, crossing over to get a better look. She hung her head over one of the pans that bubbled there. 'What exactly is in that?'

Willow came to stand beside her. 'Gooseberries, lemons, sugar and elderflower cordial. Summer in a saucepan. What do you reckon?'

'You got that right,' she agreed. 'Is that how your ice cream starts? Only much as I love that, I'd be quite happy spooning this lot up straight from the pan.'

'You wouldn't really. It smells divine, but it's very, very sweet, and very, very sticky.'

Freya looked around her once more. 'I don't think I realised quite how quickly you were going to get this all up and running. What did you do, wave a magic wand?'

'Naked incantations by the light of the moon . . . hardly . . .' Willow laughed. 'No, I waved a chocolate cake, a tub of ice cream, three punnets of strawberries and some runner beans under one of our friend's noses, and being the wondrous carpenter that he is, he put this together in an afternoon.'

'Ah, sorry,' said Freya, acknowledging the slight admonishment. 'Been reading too much Harry Potter.'

'Besides,' continued Willow, with a wink. 'That is most definitely not why you perform naked incantations by moonlight . . .' Her smile was warm as she took Freya's arm. 'And look, come and see these.'

She led the way over to the work surface where a pile of elderflowers was waiting. Beside them a muslin cloth was suspended over a large bowl, the syrupy mixture it contained slowly dripping through.

'This is my cordial. You have to steep the flower heads for twenty-four hours in the syrup before straining it, so I made this lot last night. I pretty much have to keep a batch going the whole time.'

Now that she was closer, Freya could smell the sweetness of the creamy flowers. There was nothing she liked more on a summer's day than to wander through her orchard, the sunlight glancing off the hedgerows filled with these frothy heads. She picked up a bunch and inspected it closely before bringing it to her nose. The last time she'd done this, she'd inhaled a small bug straight up her nose.

'So what do you think?' asked Willow. 'Am I mad, or do you think there's a possibility that this might work?'

Freya's head had done nothing but spin with ideas since she had left her friend at the weekend. With her and Sam's own plans for Appleyard now beginning to look like reality, this was quite possibly the most amazing opportunity for them both, and for their friend Merry too if Freya wasn't mistaken. Merry and Tom had only opened their shop a few weeks ago, and were now on the lookout for small local businesses whose produce they could showcase. The opportunity for them all to work together was serendipity indeed, and would give them the helping hand they needed to fulfil their individual dreams, of that she had no doubt.

'I think there's every possibility it will be bloody brilliant, Willow. It's a shame that Merry couldn't come today, but when I talked to her at the beginning of the week, she seemed really keen. Have you made the list of things you're hoping to produce?'

'Yes, it's on the table. Come and sit down and I'll show you.' She handed Freya a piece of paper. 'I still can't believe I didn't know that Merry had sold the hotel in Worcester and bought a shop up here; that has to be the biggest coincidence.'

'I know. It's brilliant what they've

done with it, you won't believe it until you see it.'

Freya took a few moments to read what was in front of her, and even though Willow had simply listed the products, she knew her friend well enough to know that they would all be beautifully packaged; the ice cream would be softly whipped inside smart tubs, the blackcurrant cordial would glow ruby red from glass bottles, and her gooseberry and elderflower jam would look like the pale golden glow of a winter sun. As for the smell when their lids were removed; Freya was out in the fields already. They would look perfect against her range of juices.

'I think Merry will be thrilled to stock these. I'm going to see her on Thursday, why don't you come with me? You could discuss how this could work for you both, and to be honest, Willow, I'd love to get involved. I think what we're both trying to do could be the perfect complement to each other.'

Willow smiled a little shyly. 'Are you

sure it doesn't seem a bit rude? I mean, I haven't seen Merry for ages, or much of you for that matter, and now I feel a bit like I'm throwing this all in your faces.'

'That's the way of life, Willow, we're all busy. Those strawberries out there don't grow by themselves, do they, and I certainly don't think you're being rude, and neither will Merry. In fact, far from that, I'd like to view it as a wonderful turn of fate — the perfect opportunity for all of us. Perhaps after all we make our own fate . . .'

Freya held Willow's look for a moment, recognising that she knew the truth of what she had said. Hopefully one day soon, she would find out the real reason why Willow was so keen to start this new venture. There would be a reason, there always was.

* * *

Willow sat still for quite a while after Freya had left, pondering the direction their conversation had taken, and

41

wondering whether she should confide everything. There was something different about Freya, a kindred spirit perhaps, something that despite their years of friendship she had never seen before. Freya had had a tough time last year, losing her father and what had seemed then the only hope of keeping her beloved Appleyard alive. She had come close to selling up, but now she seemed more alive than she had ever seen her, more in tune with things. Perhaps she would understand after all.

With a sudden start, the smell of the room hit her again, and she got up swiftly. She had ice cream to make, and then she must go and see Henry. She had a favour to ask.

* * *

Henry Whittaker should have been a banker or a stockbroker, or even a solicitor, anything but an artist; it just didn't suit his name. You'd only need to glance at him, though, to know that he'd never picked up a copy of the *Financial Times* in his life. If he owned any clothes other than aged, paint-splattered jeans and T-shirts, Willow had never seen them.

He was, in fact, the model tenant. He'd been with them for over two years now, coming to them with impeccable references and a firm, if paint-speckled handshake. He paid his rent on time, every month, and took great care of the property; in fact, his vegetable patch rivalled Willow's own, albeit on a smaller scale. He never had wild parties, and although Willow had made tentative enquiries, there didn't seem to be any girlfriends on the scene; or boyfriends for that matter. She often wondered in a motherly way whether he was lonely, but two energetic spaniels accompanied him wherever he went, and that seemed to be enough. As time passed, the lines in their relationship had become blurred from tenant and landlord, mainly at Henry's insistence and now Willow found it hard to look on Henry as anything other than a good friend.

Today, like most days, he was sitting at his computer, headphone wires trailing across his shirt. She'd been pulling faces through the window at him for over five minutes before he spotted her, his face creasing into a broad grin the minute he did. He waved at the door indicating that she should come in.

'That's the one thing I can never quite understand about you,' she remarked, after she'd spent a few minutes making a fuss of the dogs. 'Every time I come in here, you have headphones glued to your ears, and yet who's going to hear your music? We're too far down the road and Jude's office is right on the other side of the courtyard, even when he is there.'

Henry held out one of the headphones. 'Do you want to hear what I was listening to?' he asked, his clear grey eyes dancing with mischief.

Willow took the wire tentatively in one hand, imagining her ears being pounded by some raucous thrash metal. Instead, all she could hear was a hissing noise. 'Oh, it's stopped,' she said, but then registered his amused expression. She held the wire up again, listening to the rushing noise once more. 'What is it?' she asked. 'Some kind of weird white noise or something.'

Henry took back the headphones. 'It's pink actually. Slightly lower frequency than white noise. It helps you to concentrate, in a calm, relaxed kind of way.'

Willow pulled a face at him, and he shrugged. 'Now you know why I play it through headphones.' He grinned. He eyed the contents of the bag in her other hand.

'I sincerely hope there are strawberries in there. And I sincerely hope they're for me.'

'There's also a bribe dressed up as ice cream, so don't get too excited.'

Henry peered at her over the top of his glasses and then took them off altogether. 'Might this have something to do with our conversation from a few days ago then?'

'Possibly . . . ' admitted Willow.

'In that case, I can see this is going

to be one of those conversations that requires a cup of coffee as well,' he said. 'I'll go and fire up the beast.'

Willow looked at the bag in her hand and back to Henry's workstation. He wasn't painting today, but designing something instead; his computer screen showing half of some sort of flash racing car, but she'd still interrupted him. He was working, so she shouldn't even be here, but apart from the favour, she didn't have anyone else she could talk to about this, not yet at any rate. She bit her lip, torn.

In the end, it was Henry who decided for her, taking her arm, relieving her of the bag she was carrying, and marching her across the room to the collection of sofas and armchairs which were centred round a huge fireplace. He pushed her down into the middle of one of the settees, where she was immediately joined by a dog at her side and one at her feet. She sank back against the cushions, grateful for the opportunity to sit for a moment. So far, she had been travelling

46

through her day at a hundred miles an hour, and she suspected it would continue to be like that for several weeks to come.

After ten minutes or so of silence apart from the slurping and hissing of the coffee machine, Henry returned with two huge foamy cappuccinos which he settled on the coffee table in front of her. She smiled up at him gratefully, already feeling a little more at ease, although that may have been in part due to Dylan's heavy breathing, the beautiful blue springer spaniel, whose head was heavy in her lap.

'So what's the bribe for then?' asked Henry after a moment, licking a strip of frothy milk off his top lip. 'And before you answer, I'll remind you that I'm open to bribes of any kind where your food is considered payment.'

'Well, that's just it, the bribe is the bribe. I just want your opinion on the ice cream really . . . but —'

Henry chuckled. 'Is that all? Christ, I wish all my clients were this easy to please.' He got up and went back to the kitchen, returning with the tub of ice cream and a huge tablespoon.

'Henry, I didn't mean now! You can let me know in a day or two, when you've had time to eat it.'

He looked at her steadily. 'What is this day or two of which you speak?' He grinned and pulled off the lid, plunging his spoon into the creamy mass. It emerged with a huge dollop on the end, and he put the whole thing straight into his mouth.

Willow winced, expecting imminent brain freeze, but Henry just sat back, eyes closed, letting the sweet concoction melt in his mouth. He gave a series of swallows and then sat up once more, looking at her. He plunged the spoon in again and repeated the process. Willow said nothing.

After the third mouthful, Henry sat up straighter and lowered the spoon. 'Okay, I like it,' he said impassively.

Willow's face fell. That wasn't exactly the reaction she'd been hoping for.

'Willow,' he said, 'that was absolutely spectacular. I was just teasing!' He grinned, and she could see now that he was. He took another spoonful, smaller this time.

'I don't know how you do it,' he added. 'One minute I'm here and the next I'm out there, in the field, picking gooseberries, the sun on my arms, the insects buzzing. It's like when the fruit is so ripe and you pop one in your mouth, all the juice and seeds suddenly exploding, and then after that first tangy hit, you get the sweetness, mellow and creamy, hedgerows full of frothy elderflowers, the smell . . . I'm probably not doing it justice.'

Willow blushed. 'Really?' she asked. 'Is that what you feel? You're not just making it up?'

'No, I'm not just making it up,' he said. 'Scout's honour . . . although, I am wondering why my opinion matters so much.'

Willow reached for her coffee and took a sip, feeling Henry's eyes on her.

'I need the opinion of someone neutral. Everybody else I know is too close to home.'

'Well, I've been called many things in my time, but never "neutral" before.' He waved his spoon. 'And before you leap to apologise, I'm only teasing again. If you don't mind me saying you look really nervous, which is unusual for you . . . however, I do understand what you mean, and I'm flattered that you've asked me.' His grey eyes were smiling at her. 'Does that make you feel any better?'

Willow swallowed and nodded. 'It does actually, thanks. And you're right, I am nervous about this.' She paused for a moment, wondering how much to say, but Henry wasn't stupid, he'd have worked it out. 'You see I'm thinking that I might start making ice cream, and one or two other things, properly, you know to sell, but I've never done anything like this before, it's all a bit nerve-wracking.'

'Ah, so now we're getting to the bottom of it, but Willow, you run a fruit farm. How can you be nervous about this?'

'That's different. I don't make the fruit, it grows all by itself —'

'I think there's a bit more to it than that,' interrupted Henry, 'but perhaps I should put you out of your misery. I think what you want might be in that folder there.' He directed her towards the table with a look. 'I took the liberty of completely disregarding the cock and bull story you tried to sell me the other day, and started to mock up a few designs for you. Have a look and see whether they're what you're after. I've tried to come up with a few differing ideas, but they might be a bit too . . . masculine maybe.'

Willow's mouth hung open. 'How did you know that's what I wanted?' she managed.

'Because when someone comes in here asking me to 'doodle' a couple of pictures of some gooseberries and strawberries for you to put on a sign in your little wooden shop, and that person knows that among other things I'm a concept artist, I'm generally able to read between the lines.'

'Oh,' said Willow, a little embarrassed now. 'Was I really that obvious?'

Henry laughed. 'Have a look. I might have got it completely wrong.'

Willow pulled the folder towards her and opened it cautiously. Whatever was inside could potentially mean this thing was about to come alive, and although a part of her was ready for it, a large part of her was not.

She picked up the first piece of paper, struck first by the beautiful colour of the artwork, a soft green, like a summer meadow. Then there were pale golden hues, a gorgeous pink – the colour of the setting sun, a deep cranberry and a dark purple, the exact shade of ripe blackberries. There were bold scripts, elegant scripts and modern edgy patterns. Willow couldn't believe it. She looked up in astonishment.

'How did you do all this, it must have taken you an age?'

Henry simply smiled. 'I was on a roll,' he said. 'Do you think any of them are what you're looking for?'

Willow gazed on in wonder. 'I think they're stunning. How will I ever choose? Every one of these could make a perfect logo, and I love the way you've put them onto some packaging already. It makes them so much easier to see what they would look like.'

'It's what I do.' Henry shrugged.

A rush of excitement hit Willow like a wave. 'Can I take these away with me, to have another look? I've got a couple of friends I'd like to show them to as well, if that would be all right.'

Henry waved a hand. 'Sure, they're yours for as long as you want. They'll probably need some tweaking too, so just let me know what works and what doesn't, and we can go from there.'

'Oh my God,' squealed Willow. 'Thank you so much!' She lurched up from the sofa much to Dylan's disgust, coffee forgotten. 'I'll bring you some more ice cream,' she gushed as she rushed to the door. 'Thank you so much, Henry.'

★ ★ ★

Henry watched her go, an amused smile on his face. His hunch had been right then. He gave a sigh; time to get back to work. But then he checked his watch, picked up his spoon once more, and worked his way steadily through the entire carton of ice cream. He liked Willow, in fact he liked both of them. He'd shared a pint or two with Jude and always found him very likeable. He had pots of money of course, and a love of the finer things in life; but it rarely got the better of him. Most of the time, he appeared to be an ordinary bloke, much like himself. Only now and then had Henry seen a little seam of something darker running through him, but Jude was a very successful man, and Henry supposed it came with the territory. He wanted Willow to succeed, for her sake and, actually it was sweet that she was so reticent about her capabilities. She shouldn't be. Henry was a pretty good cook himself, but Willow was amazing. Her food was so full of flavour, so full of life. He suspected that she could make even a cardboard box taste exceptional.

* * *

It wasn't until Willow got to the bottom of the lane again that she remembered her dream. It flashed in front of her as her hand touched the gate to open it. An explosion in her mind, much like the lightning that she remembered, and she turned quickly to look behind her. The wind was filling the canopy of the trees above her, lifting the leaves in a song above her head. Beyond them there was nothing but more trees and the dusty ground of the lane which reached back towards Henry's house and the clearing where Jude also had his office. She knew that she was in the right place, though; that beyond the trees was a gentle sweep of pasture land almost as far as the eye could see, land which at the moment was a carpet of grasses and wild flowers, of hedgerows and swaying corn. It wouldn't take much to reduce it to the muddy hell hole she had seen, just a few diggers and an unhealthy greed. She shuddered, gripped by the force of the images and clutched Henry's folder to her. She had to hope that time would be on her side.

4

'How long is it since you moved here, Merry?' asked Willow. 'Only it looks like you've been here forever.'

Merry laughed. 'Well, that's only because everything is so old . . . myself included. I can't believe how tiring it is, running a shop. I thought we were busy before with the hotel, but I guess I'd forgotten how much I used to delegate,' she added ruefully. 'But it is absolutely the best fun ever. I wish we'd done it years ago.'

Willow eyed the garishly coloured fittings and decoration. 'It shouldn't work really, should it?' she commented. 'All I remember from the seventies is that it was dubbed the decade that taste forgot, but this is stunning, inspired even.'

Merry and Freya exchanged looks before Merry grinned and pointed to a rather grand portrait on the wall. 'It was inspired, actually,' she said. 'Meet Christopher, our artist in residence, his wife, Marina, and their daughter, Catherine. They're all dead by the way.'

The painting was very striking, but Willow wasn't quite sure what to make of it. It looked almost as though it had been freshly painted. 'I'm not sure I follow,' she said. 'How can he be your artist in residence if he's dead?'

'I'll tell you all about it some time,' said Merry. 'But all the work you can see on the walls is Christopher's. He was quite a well-known artist in his time; he designed wallpaper and textiles, that kind of thing. He once owned the house, and we found all these things just packed away when we moved here. It seemed right to reuse them, and they gave us the theme we were looking for.'

'It's amazing,' answered Willow. 'I love it. But you said you've still got things to do, more plans for the place?'

'We have,' said Merry. 'There are things we'd like to try, but what I'd love to show you is this little space out the back here.'

She led the way through the main part of the shop, past tables overflowing with produce, and through an archway into the rear. The smell in here was even more amazing. An array of old cupboards and bookcases lined the walls, every inch of which was covered with bottles and jars, or packets and boxes. What set these apart from the items for sale in the rest of the shop was the packaging itself and the labels. None of the items looked mass-produced, and all had an air of quality about them. The labels were classy and individual, they looked hand-lettered. It was exactly the look that Willow herself was hoping to achieve.

Willow looked about her, picking her way around the room, peering at the contents on display, and wondering whether she would be able to compete; moreover, whether anything she could produce would actually fit in here, the room was crammed to the gills as it was.

'View these as only temporary,' said Merry. 'We wanted to introduce some speciality products alongside the every-day staples we offer, but we didn't have enough time before we opened to seek out the suppliers we really wanted to use: local people with fabulous local produce. We're taking our time discovering who, and what is out there, people like you, Willow. So bit by bit, we plan to replace this lot with new lines as we find the right suppliers. What was more important in the beginning was to establish whether or not these type of products would sell, and admittedly we haven't been open that long, but people do seem to like them. I'm convinced that we'll continue to do well with them.'

'But I'm not sure how long it will be before I'm up and running,' said Willow. 'I don't want to hold you up, and I'm not sure yet what kind of quantities I'll be able to make.' She picked up a jar of bramble jelly, very similar in fact to the jars that lined her own pantry shelves at home. It was so exciting to see the possibilities of what the shop might offer her, but it also brought home just how much hard work this would involve, and what a big leap it would be for her. She still wasn't sure whether it was something she should go ahead with, but all her instincts were telling her it was. Perhaps it was the fear of what she suspected was coming next that prevented her from making the next move.

'Well, why don't we take it a step at a time,' said Merry. 'Your fruit is amazing right now, and I would certainly love to sell some for you. Can you imagine how the strawberries would smell in here? Why don't we start with some of the fruit varieties, and perhaps some bottles of your cordial, and that would give you a little more time to think about your other products, particularly the ice creams. It would also give you some time to have a play at home before you agree to provide us with anything.'

Willow didn't mean it to, but her face fell a little. She should be treading more carefully here. It wasn't that she didn't trust Merry, but this was a small community, and the village shop was the fount of all gossip. What would happen if people found out what Jude was planning before she'd had a chance to put her own plans into place? It didn't bear thinking about, but time was of the essence now.

She was just about to reply when she noticed that Freya had put down the jar of olives she was studying, and was watching her intently. It threw her for a minute, and she scrambled to say something quickly. Too late.

'Willow, is everything all right? You can tell me to mind my own business if you like, but we've been friends for too long for me not to notice when things aren't quite right. A couple of times now when we've talked about this new venture, you've seemed almost panicky, as if things weren't happening quickly enough. I mean, one minute you had a utility room, cleared out, but just a blank space, and almost the next day it was kitted out as if you were going into full production. Something doesn't quite add up here . . . ' She stopped for a moment, thinking about what she had just said.

'It's not the business, is it?' she asked quickly. 'Everything with Jude is all right?'

The question caught Willow off guard. She thought she had hidden her feelings well, but Freya had put her finger on it with unerring accuracy. To her surprise, she felt tears beginning to well up. What on earth could she say? She had no proof that her suspicions were true; they were based on dreams for heaven's sake, and to admit them out loud was tantamount to admitting she was going mad. She would also be accusing Jude before she had any facts at all. It would seem like a betrayal when all she was really trying to do was help. Just as quickly another thought came to her — a memory of a conversation with Freya in her kitchen, when she'd told her about Christmas and the stranger who had caused her to think a little differently. And here was Merry talking about a dead painter who had somehow provided her with the inspiration for her brilliant shop. Perhaps they would understand after all.

'You're going to think I'm quite mad,' she started.

Freya laughed. 'Oh, I've always known you're mad,' she said. 'But since when did that ever stop us being friends?' She smiled warmly, and when Willow looked across to Merry, she saw the same expression echoed there too.

'It's really hard to know where to start,' she began. 'Everything with the business is fine, and with Jude too; more than fine, and perhaps that's part of the problem. Despite his mother's best efforts, his father brought him up in his own image, and although Jude thankfully is nothing like Andrew in many ways, they share the same relentless materialistic streak. It's something I've always recognised in Jude, something that's always worried me a little, to tell the truth, even though for the most part he manages to keep it well in check. Even my mum warned me about it when we first got together.'

Freya came around the side of the table and perched on the corner of it.

'Actually, I always liked your mum. A bit kooky admittedly, but she always seemed so vibrant, so alive. Don't forget my own mum bailed out on us when I was only little. I loved my dad, you know that, but when I was younger, your family always seemed so happy, and I always used to think how much fun it must be to be you.'

Willow touched her hand to her mouth. 'I never knew that,' she said, eyes starting to smart again.

'Well, I'm telling you now; one, because it's true, and two, because I know you had a hard time when you were younger, kids calling your mum names just because she was a bit different to everyone else's. But looking back, all I see is a bunch of kids who never knew any better. My life has shown me, more so over the last year, that not everything that happens to us can be explained. And neither is everything black-and-white; if we allow it, life can be the most wondrous collection of colours, in every shade of the rainbow.'

Merry was nodding her head. 'I agree. The things that have happened to me over the last few months probably don't make any sense. If you ask my husband, he'd tell you a very different story. Whenever I try to tell him exactly how I feel about recent events, he gives me that weird look, you know, the one that says *you've just had a baby and your brain is still a pile of mush*. Whatever you need to tell us, I don't suppose I'll be the least bit surprised — just say it as it is.'

Willow smiled gratefully. 'A few months ago, I started to have dreams, nothing specific at first, just a vague feeling of unease. And it was at about the same time that Jude first mentioned he had a meeting up in Birmingham with his father. This alone was enough to set warning bells ringing.' She nodded at Merry. 'You probably don't know, but Andrew is still a silent partner in the business. He and Jude started Middleton Estates mostly with his capital, and even now the strawberry fields, meadowland, our house, and everything else belongs to the business. It will all transfer to Jude at some point or another of course when Andrew dies, but it's always made me feel uneasy; I feel beholden to him, even though I know he can't take any decisions without Jude's agreement. Jude has always run the company day to day, but he had a big meeting with his father at the very moment I started having my dreams. Other people might not see the significance, but to me it's like a shining beacon.'

'So what do you think is going on?' asked Freya. 'Couldn't you just ask Jude?'

'I could.' Willow paused for a moment, wondering how best to phrase her next statement. She was painfully aware that any minute she'd be laughed out of the shop. 'A couple of nights ago, I had a vision that all the land around us was completely desecrated, torn up to make room for houses. I'm convinced this is what Jude is planning, or, more likely, is an idea that his father has hatched, and Jude is going along with for some reason.

I know it makes me sound like a crazy person, but I almost don't need to know any more than that. There's no way I can talk to Jude about it, when everything I feel is based on dreams; he'd think I'm mad. So, the only thing I can think of is to offer Jude a real and valid choice, an alternative future and, importantly, a reason to go against his father's wishes.'

'Hence the new business venture?' suggested Merry.

Willow nodded sadly. 'And the need to get it up and running in far less time than is really feasible.'

Freya crossed the room to stand by her friend's side. 'Then it sounds to me like we need a hefty dose of girl power to help things along. What do you reckon, Merry? It's scary trying to do things like this on your own, and what could be more wonderful than Merry and me helping you out? Merry has the perfect place to sell your produce, plus business contacts coming out of her ears, I have some of the raw materials you need to get up and running, and I know where I can get more, and you have granny Gilly's notebook. From where I'm standing, that's a pretty powerful combination.'

Willow looked around the room one more time. All her instincts were telling her that this was the right thing to do, and they had never let her down before. Besides what other choice did she have? Her future with the man she loved, and that of her children, were at stake here. It was time to fight.

5

Willow called Peter over to see her the very next morning. It was not long since his breakfast, but despite the early hour he'd already been hard at work for a while. It would be mercilessly hot out in the fields today with no shelter, and the strawberries were much better if picked when they still held the morning's freshness.

She had a mug of tea waiting for him as he sauntered through the door, his enormous flip-flop-clad feet squeaking across her floor.

'Ah, cheers,' he said, as Willow handed him his drink. 'Is everything okay?'

Peter was one of the best students she'd ever had. Over the years they had ranged from the gormless to the adequate as long as she kept an eye on them, but Peter was different. Apart from Rachael who had been with them for the past three years, he was the only one with any initiative.

70

He was quiet and studious, with floppy brown hair and a big bushy beard, but his unobtrusive manner belied a keen intellect and a sharp wit. They got on like a house on fire. Trouble was there was only one of him, and right now Willow needed six or seven.

She gave him a bright smile. 'Wonderful,' she replied. 'How's it looking out there today?'

'Busy, and hot,' he grinned. 'But mostly hot.'

Willow looked at her watch. 'Well, let's see how it goes. If the sky stays this clear, by two the heat will be unbearable. No one will come to pick, so you must call it a day. I don't want you keeling over on me.'

Peter was six foot three and had muscles like Popeye, and his expression let her know in no uncertain terms that she was fussing, but she waggled her finger at him anyway.

'Actually, I wanted to ask a favour if that's okay? I've been having a bit of a think recently about branching out a little; making some cordials, ice creams, that sort of thing, but I'm a bit short on manpower. I don't suppose by any happy chance you have a handful of mates who'd like some work over the next day or so? They'd need to be like you, mind, not afraid of hard work.'

Peter wiped a hand across his lips as he drained the last of his tea. 'Is that what the amazing smell is all about?' he asked. 'I was wondering. Can I see?'

He crossed to the sink and rinsed his mug under the tap, upending it on the draining board before turning back to her, an endearing query on his face. Willow had no choice but to lead the way out into the hallway and into the room opposite.

It didn't take Peter long to assess what he found. He walked from one spot to the other, peering at the elderflowers, smelling the aromatic cordial and fingering the page in Willow's notebook where her grandma had carefully written the recipe in her best copperplate handwriting.

'So you need people to pick? And in

huge quantities by the look of things. Maybe people to man the strawberry fields, and possibly people in here to keep the pans going?'

Willow smiled, watching Peter carefully.

'Leave it to me,' he beamed, with a glance out of the window. 'Right, time I was back out there I reckon.' He looked back at the room as he passed through the door. 'Would the day after tomorrow be okay?'

* * *

Willow was right, by the time two o'clock came, the strawberry field was scorching. In fact, everywhere was scorching, but that had its advantages too. The picked fruit had marched out of the door during the morning, but actual pickers were reluctant to venture out which gave Willow the perfect opportunity to shut up shop early and pop over to see Henry. She had pored over his designs the night before, and every time she picked up the folder, she found herself returning to one particular set of designs. The colours were striking, a vibrant lime green and a deep pinky-plum, and although the motifs and lettering were modern, there was something timeless about them too. She was sure that they would appeal to the market she was aiming at.

It was much cooler in the shaded lane and she walked slowly, taking the time to trail her fingers through the fronds of cow parsley along the verge, and inhale the gentle scent from the wild sweet peas which grew there.

Henry was in the garden when she arrived, standing among the tomatoes and sweet peppers which he'd planted to take full advantage of the warmth from the red brick wall that ran the length of one side. He waved a greeting.

'Warm enough for you?' he called, straightening up, one hand full of sweet cherry tomatoes.

'Only just,' she replied. 'But alas too hot for my pickers. Most of them have sloped off to a deckchair and a glass of

Pimms, so I thought I'd come and har-
ass you instead.'

'Lucky old me.' He grinned. 'Go on
in, I won't be a minute. Dinner won't
pick itself.'

Willow glanced at the array of vegetables and herbs in front of her. Whatever
Henry was planning for his tea, she had
no doubt it would be tasty. She followed
the path to the wide French doors, both
open, stepping over the two panting
spaniels who were sprawled in the shade
cast by the house.

Inside, the living room was cool and
dark, and she took a seat, admiring Henry's artwork on the walls. All was quiet
for a moment until the sound of a door
opening caused her to look up.

A young woman stood in the entrance
to the room, quite naked.

'Oh, hi,' she said, stepping into the
room and looking around. 'Does Henry
know you're here? I could fetch him if
you like.' She made no move to cover
herself.

Willow was never very good at judging

75

people's age, but the lithe tanned body in front of her could be no more than early twenties.

Willow cleared her throat. 'Sorry. I met him in the garden. He said to come on in . . .'

'Okay,' she said with a smile, looking down at her feet as if seeing them for the first time. Funnily enough, her feet were not what was concerning Willow. 'I should probably go and get dressed. Aren't you hot?'

Willow managed a smile. 'A bit,' she said cautiously.

The young woman stared at her as if she was deranged, and with a nod and another smile disappeared back though the door.

'Right, so a cup of tea, is it?' asked Henry coming inside. 'Or something cold?' He was carrying a trug full of salad vegetables.

Willow was still staring at the door in the corner of the room, feeling hotter than ever.

Henry followed her line of sight.

'Ahhh,' he said slowly. 'I can see you've met Delilah.'

Willow gazed at him. 'Delilah?'

He nodded. 'As in *Why, Why, Why Delilah* . . . You know, the Tom Jones song?'

'I can see *why* Delilah, Henry, she's gorgeous . . . I just didn't expect —'

'She wasn't wearing any clothes, was she?' Henry grinned. 'She does that. She's a goat keeper,' he added, as if that explained it.

Willow remained seated, hoping for further explanation, but as Henry hopped from foot to foot, it became clear that it wasn't going to arrive any time soon.

'Henry Whittaker, you're a dark horse,' she said in her best school matron's voice. 'And don't tell me she's your sister; nobody has a sister like that.'

'No, she's not my sister.' He laughed. 'She's not my niece either.'

'So are you going to tell me what's going on, or not?' she retorted, getting up from the chair. 'This is the first time I've seen another female anywhere remotely near here, so don't go all shy on me now.'

Henry blushed a little. 'I'll go and put the kettle on.'

Ten minutes later, the three of them were sitting around the kitchen table, Delilah now ever so slightly dressed in a skimpy pair of shorts and vest top. She sat cross-legged in the chair, cradling her mug in her lap.

'So how did you two meet?' asked Willow. 'You're rather a long way from home if I'm right in thinking that's a Cornish accent.'

'You are,' smiled Delilah, 'but where I'm from, everywhere is a long way from home. I spend my life on the M5.'

'I can imagine. So . . .?'

Henry shared an amused glance across the table with Delilah. 'This might explain it,' he said, throwing his foot up onto the empty chair next to Willow. He rolled up the leg of his jeans to reveal bright green socks. 'Goat socks,' he said. 'At this precise moment I have about eighteen pairs, which is sixteen pairs more than I actually need.'

Delilah poked Henry's thigh. 'But you have to admit that the after sales service is spectacularly good . . .'

Henry sighed. 'It is . . . which is why I have eighteen pairs.'

'Oh, I see.' Willow giggled.

'We actually only met for the first time about three months ago,' adds Henry. 'Up until then, I'd ring Delilah to order another pair of socks and heave and sigh listening to her talk dirty to me in that fabulous accent —'

'While I would swoon listening to his cut glass vowels . . . in the end, I decided that although the poor man was pretty much keeping me in business, enough was enough, so I suggested we meet —'

'And the rest is history,' finished Henry.

Willow felt like a spectator at a tennis match, as she struggled to keep up with the conversation that batted back and forth, Henry and Delilah both finishing each other's sentences.

'Well, it's lovely to meet you, Delilah, although I shall thump Henry later for not telling me about you. How long are you staying for? Only if you're here for a few days, then you should come over to us for dinner one evening. I haven't cooked properly for anyone in ages.'

Henry exchanged another look with Delilah before replying. 'Willow runs a fruit farm,' he explained, 'but she also happens to be the finest cook for miles around, *and* she makes the most amazing ice cream.'

'To be honest, I'm not entirely sure how long I'll be here for,' replied Delilah with a rather coy look at Henry. 'We're sort of taking things as they come . . . dinner sounds a lovely idea, though, thank you.' She twiddled the ends of her jet black hair around her fingers. 'I don't suppose you make your ice cream with goat's milk, do you?'

'No, sorry,' replied Willow. 'It's rather a new venture. I think I need to stick with what I know for now, but who knows, maybe one day.' She suddenly felt very naïve in front of this confident young woman who obviously had a successful business herself. There was so much she needed to learn.

She sat up a little straighter in her chair. 'Actually, Henry, I'm sorry for hogging your afternoon, but the ice cream making is the reason I popped round. I've made a decision on the designs you produced for me, but I'm not sure where to go from here. I need packaging and marketing stuff, but I'm clueless about who to use, and what it's likely to cost. I was hoping you might be able to point me in the right direction.'

Henry's grey eyes sparkled at her. 'But that's brilliant news, Willow. Which designs did you go for in the end?' He got up from the table. 'Hang on and I'll get my laptop.'

It took a few moments for him to boot it up and navigate to the right folder, but almost immediately Delilah pulled her chair closer to his so that she could see the screen too. 'I've got Henry working on some new designs for me as well, but I'd love to see what else he's been doing. Frankly, I'm amazed he even found my company to begin with, my website is so out of date it's shocking, and while the stuff I produce is of the highest quality, the designs for the packaging and branding are total pants.' She looked at the screen for a moment as Henry scrolled through the images, her hand suddenly grabbing his to halt the movement. 'Oh, I like those ones,' she exclaimed. 'The colours are wonderful, and —'

She suddenly stopped, looking across at Willow, misreading her expression. 'Sorry,' she said. 'I get a bit excitable sometimes.'

Willow could feel a little tingle in her toes. 'Do you really like them?' she urged, 'only that set is the one I've picked. I could have one colour for each of the different flavours. So my elderflower ice cream and cordial could have this zingy green for example and —'

'Maybe this for strawberry?' finished Delilah.

The two women stared at one another for a moment, beaming smiles on both their faces. Willow's hand strayed to the tiger's eye pendant around her neck, where it remained, her fingers stroking the smooth polished surface of the stone.

'That's exactly what I was going to say,' said Willow. 'I don't suppose you know someone who makes brilliant, but not too expensive packaging, do you?'

Delilah gave Henry a gentle nudge to the ribs. 'Any chance of a biscuit my gorgeous lover,' she said in a thick Cornish drawl, 'an' we might be needing some more tea an all,' she added, blowing a kiss. 'Willow and I have a lot to talk about.'

6

'I hope we're not too early,' said Peter, looking at Willow's astonished face. 'Only I wasn't sure how long this would take.'

She swallowed her mouthful of tea. 'No, not too early. I just . . . didn't expect quite so many of you,' replied Willow. 'But this is wonderful!' she finished, doing a swift tally in her head. Where on earth had Peter dredged all these people up from? And more importantly people who all looked pleased to be here.

'So who have we got?' she asked. 'Although I should apologise in advance because I'll probably forget half your names in the next five minutes.'

'Okay, so we have Callum, my brother,' Peter began, 'followed by Luke and Josh, twins obviously. Jennie, who's Josh's girl-friend, Lucy her friend, and Ollie. I can vouch for them all except Ollie, who's a drunken reprobate most of the time, but

84

has promised to be on his best behaviour today.'

Willow had a feeling he was joking, but she wasn't entirely sure. She smiled, a little nervously. 'Right, well . . . have you all had breakfast?' A chorus of affirmation followed.

'And they've all got plenty to drink, snacks to eat and are smothered in factor 50.'

'Peter, what would I do without you?'

Willow downed the rest of her tea as fast as possible and snatched an apple from the bowl on the table. 'Right, do you want to follow me, and we'll get going? I'll explain what I need once we're outside, and then you can decide what you want to do.'

In the end, it was an easy decision. Peter declared that he was a strawberry man. It was what he knew, and he could help the others if they got stuck. He picked his 'team' of Callum, Ollie and Luke, leaving Josh, Jennie and Lucy to stay with Willow. After a few moments of discussion, Peter led his crew away, and

Willow watched him stride out into the field with pride. She and her strawberries were in safe hands.

She led the others around to the side of the house and one of the long low barns that stood there. At the moment, it was mainly used for storage of outdoor equipment, but Willow had other plans for it long term. Inside it was dark and still, a warm musty smell rushing through the opened door, dust motes spilling out into the sunshine. Inside, she quickly found what she was looking for and brought the special hods over for everyone to see.

'I bought these a while ago from a market selling old farm equipment,' Willow explained. 'They're actually for picking apples, but perfect for all sorts of things.' She showed them the large bucket made from canvas and reinforced with metal strips. A wide canvas strap was attached at each side. 'You wear them across your body. They're surprisingly comfortable, and you get both hands free for picking, plus you don't have to keep bending down. I've only got two, though, so we'll have to share.'

'No problem,' said Josh. 'Jennie and I can share.'

'Great! I'll wear the other one, and let's get going, shall we? The elderflower's only in the next-door field, so it's not far.'

She stopped when they got to the hedgerow, and turned to face the group. 'I'm just going to point this out,' she started, 'because it's not as daft as it sounds, and definitely not 'cause I think you're all thick.' She held a frond of creamy white flowers in her hand. 'So this is cow parsley.' She then reached overhead to pluck another head of flowers from the bush above her. 'While this, on the other hand, is elderflower, and they are actually pretty similar.' She shook the head of elderflowers. 'And whereas this one makes a gorgeous fresh tasting drink, cow parsley tastes revolting. It also looks very similar to Hemlock which if you're unlucky enough to eat will kill you.'

She smiled reassuringly at Lucy who was beginning to look a little nervous. 'Fortunately, although the flowers look quite similar, the leaves on the elderflower are quite different . . . look.' She showed them the rounded leaves on the bush above her. 'So I know you'll all be fine, and since I like nothing more than to tease my husband who once picked a fine crop of both for me, I'm counting on you three not to let me down.' She grinned. 'We're also only going to pick half the flowers on each bush. That way we leave the other half to turn into beautiful elderberries come the autumn.'

'Are those the tiny purple berries that people make into wine?' asked Jennie. 'My grandad used to give it to us at Christmas. It was revolting.'

Willow laughed. 'I think they've had rather a bad press as far as homemade wine goes, but I make them into a cordial which is gorgeous, and a pretty fearsome liqueur too. Has you under the table in a matter of minutes if you're not used to it.'

By the time Willow even thought to check her watch again, nearly three hours had passed amid much happy chatter, laughter and the odd Taylor Swift song belted out from Jennie's iPod. Above her the sun continued to beam down on them as the skylark's distinctive call filled the air, and cabbage white butterflies danced to find their dinner. There was nowhere finer to be on a summer's day, and if this was work, Willow hoped she could do it forever. She'd lost count of the number of times the hods had been emptied into the plastic sacks she'd also brought along, and now half a dozen were full and ready to take back to the house.

She motioned for everyone to join her, taking off her hat, and shielding her eyes from the sun.

'Look at this lot, amazing!' she exclaimed. 'Thank you all so much. You've all worked so hard.'

She was met with three happy faces.

'Why don't we take these back to the house, and I can get you all some lunch?

I made a special treat for pudding.'

The two girls exchanged grins. 'I've really enjoyed this morning, Willow,' said Lucy. 'I didn't think it would be half as much fun as it has been, and it's so beautiful here.'

Willow smiled to herself. Lucy who at first had been a little shy, and quieter than the other two, had soon relaxed in the fragrant air, with the sun warming her limbs and the light breeze ruffling her hair. Willow had seen it so many times before, but the magic of the countryside never lost its potency. She gave a slight shiver, acknowledging the dark clouds that hovered just out of sight, but she pushed them away. That was a battle for another day.

Having sent Josh out to fetch Peter and the other lads, she and Lucy poured out some drinks, while Jennie laid the table. It was simple food, but once it covered the table, the comments were full of appreciation. A fresh cob loaf stood in the centre, surrounded by a wedge of strong cheese, ripe tomatoes — the size of small apples — and a dish of plum chutney which glowed pinky-red in the sunlight. A huge strawberry Pavlova sat waiting to one side, a jug of fresh cream beside it. Mouths watered, plates were heaped, and bellies were filled. It was the perfect end to a perfect morning.

Willow looked up at the big clock that hung on the wall behind the table and then back down at the sea of contented faces. There were still a couple of hours to go before the children got home from school.

'Right then, who'd like to pick some gooseberries this afternoon?'

★ ★ ★

It wasn't unusual for Jude to get home from work late when he was away from the office. The clients who bought the huge estates his company sold were wealthy and liked to be wined and dined as part of the deal. Sometimes, they just liked to talk, about their holidays or their yachts, their art collection or the shares they'd just sold for a couple of million. Jude would do whatever it took to get the business, but he always let Willow know when he was going to be delayed. Always.

She hadn't even realised how late it was until her stomach gave a huge gurgle. Lovely though it had been, lunch was a distant memory, and now the girls were already in bed, and the quick half hour she had planned checking the elderflowers over before dinner had turned into nearly an hour.

With a sigh, she covered her precious crop and went back through to the kitchen. Her mobile phone still lay on the table, and she checked it again. The last message she had received from Jude was at six thirty, saying he would be home in about an hour. Whilst in reality this meant it would be nearer eight before he got in, it was now nearly nine. She opened the Aga's warming drawer and peered at the lasagne. It was now or never.

By the time she had finished her food,

a curl of unease was working its way up her spine. This was not like Jude at all, and all her calls to his mobile had gone straight to his answerphone. She didn't know what to do. This had never happened before, and there was no one she could contact. He worked alone day to day, and although his father was a partner in the business, he would have no more idea about Jude's whereabouts than she did. Besides which, she would rather wait, alone and anxious, before she called that man. She drew up her legs on the kitchen chair, wrapping her arms around them. She would wait until ten o'clock, and then she was calling the police.

The room was fully dark when the sweep of headlights hit the wall opposite her. It was three minutes to ten. Willow let out a breath and rose stiffly from the chair, one leg refusing to work after being bent in the same position for so long. She resisted the urge to fly down the hallway. Whatever had detained Jude would not be helped by her ranting at him like a hysterical fishwife, but it would take all her acting powers to remain calm and reasoned.

Any anger she had, however, evaporated the minute she caught sight of him. At first, she thought he'd been in a fight; his clothes were dishevelled, his tie gone altogether. But then she saw the expression on his face and the breath caught in her throat. Like anybody, Jude had days when his mood was not as sunny as on others, but in all the years they'd been together she'd never seen him look so low, utterly defeated in fact. He looked as if he were barely hanging on by a thread, and then he turned away from her gaze, as if ashamed.

He carried no bag, no paperwork, no phone or iPad; all the things he had left the house with that morning and, as Willow followed him slowly up the stairs, he might as well have been a ghost for all the substance he had. She flicked on the bedroom light ahead of him, darting in front to try and engage with him in some way, but he turned a weary head towards her.

'Please Willow, don't. Just come to bed. Just be with me.'

By the time she had turned off the lights downstairs and locked up for the night, Jude was already in bed. His once immaculate suit lay discarded in a heap by the bed, only the watch she had given him the Christmas before was placed carefully on the table beside the bed.

She slipped on her pyjamas and crawled into bed beside him where he pulled her so that she lay almost on top of him, her blonde hair splayed out in a fan across his naked chest. He began to stroke it, and it was a long time before his hand finally stilled and he slept. Willow closed her eyes and waited.

7

Jude had got up as usual at seven o'clock that morning, spent double the amount of time he normally did in the bathroom, and emerged as if nothing had happened the evening before. He ate wholemeal toast and honey like he always did, drank a cup of tea, followed by a cup of coffee as was his custom, and it wasn't until Willow sat pointedly in front of him that he looked up with a grimace.

'Oh God, that's better. I feel almost human again,' he said with a wry smile. 'Remind me never to entertain Mr Nakamura and his cronies again. They took me to some 'authentic' restaurant, and I've never felt so ill in all my life. I ate things that would probably make me feel sick just looking at them, never mind having them for dinner. Coupled with some heinous wine concoction. I'm a country boy at heart, I can't cope with too much exotica.'

Willow studied him for a moment, his face open and honest, just like it always was. He looked a little tired, but the desolation of the night before was nowhere to be seen.

'I'm really sorry I didn't let you know I'd be so late. Events overtook me rather, and the Japanese consider it extremely rude to use your phone in a restaurant. I was in a bit of a quandary really.'

'You could have called when you left the restaurant. I was really worried.'

'Willow, I was completely pickled. I was way over the legal limit and not thinking logically about anything. I can't believe I drove home.' He shuddered. 'It doesn't bear thinking about.'

He reached out his hand to her. 'Listen, I'm back in the office today, and there's every chance I could be finished by three. Why don't we take the girls and go out for a picnic tea?'

It was a lovely idea, and were it not for the fact that she was absolutely sure that not one drop of alcohol had passed her husband's lips last night, she would have accepted his peace offering without a second thought. His story was so convincing he even had himself believing it, but there was more to it than that; a lot more. Willow didn't need second sight to know that her husband needed her more than ever right now. Whatever was happening in his world, he was trying to shield her from it, just as he always did, only this time it was serious. This time he was scared.

* * *

Jude kissed his wife goodbye and left the house by the back door. He closed his eyes momentarily against the bright sunlight, and took a deep breath before continuing the short walk to his office. He wasn't sure that he had completely got away with it, but Willow was not the suspicious kind, and she was worried about him rather than looking to find some darker reason for his behaviour yesterday. With any luck by this evening, she would have forgotten about it entirely. Jude, however, was certain that the events of the previous evening would stay with him for a long time to come.

* * *

Willow hoped Peter wouldn't notice the bags under her eyes, although knowing him, he would and just wouldn't say anything. Now more than ever, it seemed important to get her new venture well and truly underway. She was beginning to feel panicked, which was not like her at all, but last night had spooked her. She had never seen Jude look so distraught, and the fact that he had lied so blatantly about what had happened was proof enough that something was very amiss.

She stood in the doorway to her new stillroom, hands on her hips surveying the stacked crates of elderflowers, and the bags full of flower heads that had yet to be checked over. There was so much to do and the only way through it was to start at the beginning and work methodically. She picked up three huge boiling pans in succession, filling each with water and setting them to heat.

'Peter, would you mind paring the zest from all these lemons, and then quarter the fruit when you've done that?'

He stared at the huge pile of waxy fruit on the table. 'Good job I've got no paper cuts,' he quipped.

Willow was weighing out quantities of sugar. 'Just don't pare your fingers at the same time as the zest,' she grimaced, 'then you'll know about it.'

'So, what exactly is it that we're doing here?' asked Peter. 'Talk me through it from beginning to end.'

Not only was Peter super-efficient, he was a fast learner, and as Willow explained how she made her cordial, she knew she would only have to tell him once.

He nodded in understanding. 'And how much are we making exactly?' he asked, eyeing up the syrup from a previous batch dripping through a muslin cloth into the bowl below.

'If I say until the elderflowers run out, promise me you won't run away.'

Peter stared at her impassively. 'Something tells me you don't just mean that pile of elderflowers there.'

Willow wrinkled her nose. 'Pretty much the whole field, and maybe the next one too . . .'

'I see. And how many lemons would we need for that?'

She crossed the room to the tall fridge standing in one corner and pulled open the door. A mass of bright yellow ovals covered every shelf. She closed the door quickly.

Peter sighed and picked up the zester, peering at the lemon in his hand.

'One . . .' he intoned, but when Willow risked a glance at him, he was smiling.

The morning passed in a blur of lemon-scented industry, until the last of the elderflowers had been checked over for bugs and stacked in the waiting crates, and every work surface held pan after pan of the summery concoction. They could do no more until tomorrow when the syrup was ready to be strained.

Willow, however, was not finished with the day yet.

'Do you want to make some ice cream?' She grinned.

Peter, who had a glass of water halfway to his lips, nearly choked before he had even begun to drink it.

'Now might not be the best time to mention that I don't actually like ice cream,' he said.

Willow grinned. 'In that case now might be the perfect time to mention that that doesn't matter in the slightest. Besides, I'll soon change your mind.'

She enjoyed the teasing banter she shared with Peter. He was easy to talk to, but he never let their chatter get in the way of hard work. The morning had taken her mind off the images of last night; not removed them but pushed them firmly enough to one side so that she was able to concentrate on the task at hand. She had to stay focused now. She had to be smart if this venture was ever going to succeed, and simply making gorgeous cordials or ice creams wouldn't be enough. She wasn't just trading in yet another food stuff; instead, she was selling the hum of summer hedgerows, busy with bees, the feeling of sun on bare toes whilst walking country lanes, the soft quiet dawn turning to the pale violet close of the day. It was everything she held dear, bottled, packaged and enticing. She was selling the dream. And not only was she selling it, but she also had to convince some pretty important people that they wanted to buy it.

She glanced back at Peter who had now finished his drink and was waiting for further instructions. He had asked nothing of her during the morning, beyond the odd check that he was doing things correctly, or what to do next, but she could sense his curiosity. It was pretty obvious, particularly to someone with Peter's intellect that her comment about branching out her business a little was not all there was to it, but she still wasn't sure how much she should confide in him. She trusted him, that wasn't the issue, but how did you explain to someone that everything you were doing, every decision you made was because of a feeling, a hunch, even a bad dream. It sounded kooky even to her.

She took some cream from the fridge. 'The ice cream isn't difficult to make,' she said. 'It's basically gooseberry puree mixed with elderflower cordial and added to whipped cream, but I find it has a happy spot when you're mixing. It's hard to explain, but under or over the happy spot and it doesn't seem quite the same somehow. I'll try and —'

Willow was interrupted by the sound of her mobile ringing. She glanced down at the table, her face crossed with anxiety when she noted who the caller was. She picked the phone up immediately.

'Maggie, is everything okay?'

She listened, nodding, for a few seconds, her expression growing more and more concerned. 'I'll come straight away. I can be with you in about ten minutes . . . Is Amy okay? She'll be so upset about her sister.'

Peter looked up sharply when he heard Amy's name mentioned and his eyes connected with Willow's as she lowered the phone.

'That was the school,' she murmured, her hand fluttering to her throat. 'Beth fell awkwardly in PE, they think she might have broken her arm.'

Peter took the phone from her hand with a glance at his watch. 'Go and get your bag and keys. I'll ring Jude, maybe he can pick Amy up later, otherwise I'll go.' He shooed her out of the room, already dialling the number. By the time she returned, it was all sorted, and he pushed the phone back into Willow's hands.

'Go on, go. We'll look after everything here until you get back. Just keep in touch, let us know how you get on, okay? And give my love to Beth.'

Willow gave him one final look before turning on her heel. Her mind was already elsewhere.

★ ★ ★

Peter watched her retreating back as she hurried down the hallway. It was every parent's worst nightmare, and he hoped that Beth was okay. He'd never really had any experience with children before coming to work for Willow, but Beth was bright as a button, and funny too. She'd had him in stitches one day trying to teach him tongue twisters. She was so much better at them than he was. Amy was quieter than her twin, a little more thoughtful perhaps, but just as adorable, and she would miss her sister dreadfully this afternoon. He didn't think he had ever seen them apart.

He turned back to the table and looked at the two large pots of cream that Willow had put there moments earlier. The navy-blue notebook lay a little distance away, and he picked it up thoughtfully. He'd never made ice cream before, but maybe this would help to keep him occupied while he waited for news about Beth. After all, how hard could it be?

The gooseberries were cooling by the time Peter heard the back door slam, and the sound of running feet. He knew that Amy would head for the kitchen first, and as he pulled open the door to the stillroom, he was met with her tear-stained face racing down the hallway to find him. She barrelled into his legs just as a tired-looking Jude came through the door. He looked a little fraught.

'I want to go to the hospital.' Amy wailed into his legs. He suspected Jude had heard nothing else since he picked her up from school, but he bent down as close as he could to her level, pulling her gently away so that he could at least see her face.

'I'm sure you do,' he said. 'I know if it were my sister that had hurt her arm, that's exactly what I'd like to do too.'

The tears halted for a moment. 'Then why can't I go? Daddy says I can't go.'

Peter took hold of her hand and started to lead her back down the hallway. He bent down to whisper in her ear.

'Shall I tell you what I think? I think daddy doesn't want you to go because then he'll have no one to look after him while Beth and mummy are at the hospital. Daddies get scared too, you know.'

Amy looked up at him, her blue eyes large and round. 'But you could look after him.'

Peter bit back a sigh, thinking quickly. 'But I'm looking after you,' he said.

There was silence for a moment while Peter was subjected to rigorous scrutiny by the six-year-old still holding his hand.

'Okay,' she replied. 'I'll look after daddy then . . . Do you think he'll want a biscuit?'

Peter grinned. 'I'm sure he will. I think he'll also like a very strong cup of coffee,' he added, with a quick look at Jude. 'But I can make that. You go and see if there're any jammy dodgers left.'

Amy skipped off happily to the kitchen while Peter smiled at Jude apologetically. 'Sorry about that,' he murmured. 'Best I could come up with at short notice.'

Jude looked exhausted, but he laid a hand on Peter's shoulder. 'No, thank you,' he smiled. 'Jammy dodgers . . . blimey, I haven't had one of those in years.

Are they still as good as I remember?'

Peter nodded. 'Best get in there before they all go. I'll put the kettle on.' He followed Jude into the kitchen where Amy was already sitting at the table, biscuit tin in front of her.

'You know what, Ames,' said Jude, sitting down. 'I'm rubbish at drawing things. Would you help me make a get-well card for Beth? I think she'd like that.'

Amy shot Peter an exasperated look. 'Daddy, Beth won't want a rubbish card, will she? *I'll* make the card, and you can help.'

Peter turned away quickly so that she wouldn't see his smile.

Leaving the two of them at the table surrounded by card and felt tip pens, Peter went back to the stillroom wondering whether he had the nerve to finish making the ice cream. He'd read through the instructions in the notebook several times but was still baffled. *Mix together the whipped cream and gooseberry puree until it starts to sing* — what on earth did that mean?

He washed his hands and pushed a tentative finger into the gooseberries that he'd left to cool. Perfect. He checked the recipe again and then took up a bowl in a meaningful manner.

So far so good. He was now staring at a bowl full of whipped cream and one of gooseberry puree, mixed with the fragrant elderflower cordial. He picked up the second bowl, stared at the wooden spoon in his hand, and started to pour.

At first, the gooseberry puree cut swirls of green through the cream, but as his spoon moved back and forth, they began to turn a pale-yellow colour. He mixed some more, energetically this time and was rewarded with a higher pitched sound than before. It wasn't quite singing yet, but Peter could hear the difference and that was all the encouragement he needed. After a few more minutes, he stopped. The recipe was right. Some strange alchemy indeed, but if he had to choose a word to describe it, he would have said that the ice cream was happy, singing away in the bowl as he mixed.

He'd already laid out a plastic container on the table, and now he moved it a bit closer, grinning with delight as he poured out his first batch of ice cream. He placed it reverently in the freezer, and sat back down at the table, a hum of excitement settling with him. He had done it.

Willow rang again just after seven. She sounded tired but relieved as she explained that they would soon be on their way home. The doctor had declared that no bones were broken, but Beth had sprained her arm, and it would still be sore for a few days. Now all she wanted to do was get home and snuggle up in bed with Matilda, her favourite bear.

Peter exchanged a look with Jude. He had stayed, not only to help look after Amy, but because he didn't want to leave without knowing what had happened to Beth. Now it was time for the family to be together again, and he didn't want to outstay his welcome. He dropped a kiss on Amy's head, telling her he would see her tomorrow and let Jude walk him to the door. He'd never really thought about his life in terms of being a father before, and yet the few hours he had spent with Amy and Jude had convinced him that at some point in his life, there was nothing he would like better. He'd only ever seen Jude when he was coming or going, never for long enough to form an opinion beyond the fact that he was a bit of a flash merchant. He knew he worked hard for his family, but the clothes he wore were just that bit too nice for Peter's taste, the car he drove, just that bit too arrogant. But tonight, he'd seen a different person in Jude. He'd seen the person who wanted nothing more than to make his daughter happy.

* * *

Jude closed the door thoughtfully. He'd never really paid any of the students who came to help Willow much attention before. They went almost as soon as they arrived, and although he was on hand if there was ever a problem, Willow seemed to manage them perfectly well without his help. Peter was different though, and he let his thoughts meander through the various scenarios he now had in his head. He wouldn't discuss any of them with Willow however, not just yet.

With an ear cocked, listening out for Amy, he pushed open the door to the stillroom, a place about which Willow had said very little recently. He admitted that in the past he'd rarely ventured inside. It was more Willow's domain than his, and unless she wasn't around and he needed to find something, what reason did he ever have to go in there? Things had changed, though. There was a bustle about the place that he had only just allowed to register. Smells that, although he was used to them, seemed to be occurring more frequently. Willow didn't keep secrets but neither had she volunteered much about what she'd been up to lately.

He hadn't thought about what he would find as he entered the room, but he was transfixed by what he saw. A slow smile began to turn up the corners of his mouth as he stared around him. He had gone through hell last night. It had been far worse than he had ever imagined and afterwards he had sat for hours, practically motionless trying to remind himself that what he was doing was the right thing. He had crawled home to bed, and to Willow, who was all he had craved, but the cost of what he had done would be his to bear for a long time yet. This was good, though. This was a glimmer of hope for the road ahead, and Willow was in for such a surprise.

8

'Peter, I could kiss you!' exclaimed Willow, grinning, as he backed away in embarrassment. 'Don't worry,' she added, 'I was only joking, you're quite safe! This is perfect, though. It tastes wonderful . . . ' She winked at him. 'Almost as good as I could make myself.'

The tub of ice cream lay on the table in front of them, a spoon sticking out of its depths.

'I was a bit mystified by the thought of it singing to me, but bizarrely, once I'd got to that point, it did seem to make sense. I might have been dreaming, though.'

'That's grandma Gilly's notebook for you,' she replied. 'It's full of all things magical.'

Peter didn't doubt that it was. He eyed the silver moon on the corner of the cover. He'd had a little peek at the pages beyond the instructions for the ice cream, and some of the 'recipes' were certainly not for things you'd want to eat . . .

'So, what's next?' he asked. 'In the grand scheme of things, I mean.'

Willow made a face. 'It's not a very grand scheme at all. In fact, I'm making most of it up as I go along.'

She laid down the pencil she was doodling with. It was another hot day, and her long hair was loosely wound into two plaits. She blew a puff of air upwards, trying to ruffle the line of her fringe. 'I should have a plan, shouldn't I?' she asked. 'I should have all this laid out like a military campaign, so I know exactly what I'm doing.'

Peter pulled the spoon from the ice cream, a generous dollop still attached to it which he made no effort to remove. Instead, he stuck the whole thing in his mouth and closed his eyes, letting the ice cream melt and trickle around his mouth. A small dribble escaped.

He opened one eye. 'Am I now wearing this?' He sighed, knowing that his beard had mopped up any excess.

Willow giggled. 'We should really put this back into the freezer.' She held out her hand for the spoon, which Peter offered up reluctantly.

'Do I take it that you now like ice cream?' she asked.

Peter ignored her. 'So tell me what it is you want to accomplish. Really accomplish, that is. Rather than what you're pretending, which is that you're just fooling around making a few pots of ice cream here and there.'

Willow picked up the tub of ice cream and got up from the table without saying a word. Peter thought at first he'd upset her, but when she turned back from the freezer she had a gentle smile on her face.

'I am *so* not a businesswoman,' she said. 'I mean, look at me. Bare feet, plaits, and a smock. And yes, before you say it, I know I run a fruit farm, but that's different. I don't have to convince anyone to eat the strawberries, or gooseberries or whatever, people do it all by themselves. I don't change the product in any way, after all, why mess with perfection? I simply grow the fruit, and people come and buy it.'

'I'm sure it's not quite as cut and dried as that,' interrupted Peter. 'You need to know what you're doing for one thing,' he added.

'That's very kind of you, but really Mother Nature does most of it.' She paused, gathering her thoughts. 'What I want is a business that's sustainable all year round. I want to gather everything we have here, and take it out there . . .' she waved a vague hand at the window, ' . . . to people who don't have these gorgeous things on their doorstep, who don't get up every morning and gaze out on fields sparkling with the morning dew. Who aren't as lucky as we are. I want to share it, but in the process I want to give our family a future, here on this land, so that it never has to become a field full of houses, or offices or a car park. That's actually the most important thing to me, but I'm not stupid enough to think that we don't need money to survive, or to grow, and I know people won't want to buy the things I make just because I say they're good. I'll need to convince them . . . I just don't know how.'

She sat down at the table with a thump. 'I have ideas for all the things I want to make, I know how to make them. I have someone who makes packaging to put them in, and I have designs for said packaging. I just don't have a bloody clue about what to do next. How to get it out there.'

Peter rubbed the end of his nose. 'And this business?' he began, 'how big is it going to be? Are we talking about shed loads of investment? New premises? Staff?'

Willow snorted. 'God no. Just enough for us, our family, no more. Small, selective, self-sufficient, an extension of our lives here. We have the space and if we need somewhere a little bigger to work from, there're always the barns outside. I grow a lot of what we eat . . . and we can live pretty cheaply really. We don't need masses of money . . . we never have.'

Now we're getting to the heart of the matter, thought Peter, watching her expression. 'So start-up costs are relatively small. You've sourced your equipment. You have a worthy range of products, now what you need is marketing and exposure, would that be right?'

Willow eyed him cautiously.

'Only it strikes me that you have what you need right under your nose, and I'm wondering why you haven't asked him.'

Peter might be mistaken, but he thought he detected a slight blush at his words.

'Ask who?' replied Willow. 'Oh, do you mean you? That would be perfect, Peter, I —'

He held up his hand. 'No, I don't mean me . . . although I do almost have a degree in Business and Management. I meant Jude actually. He's a salesman, isn't he?'

'Well, not really,' frowned Willow. 'That makes it sound like he sells double glazing . . . not that there's anything wrong with that of course,' she added quickly. 'But what Jude does is a bit different. He sells land, huge farms, estates, I mean he even sold an island once. He has a very specialist knowledge, and . . . ' She caught sight of Peter's stony expression and ground to a halt. 'Yes, at the end of the day I guess he is a salesman,' she accepted.

'So what's the problem, Willow?' asked Peter softly. 'Why won't you talk to him about any of this? And don't say it's because it's a stupid idea and he wouldn't want to be bothered with it.'

'Okay then, I won't.'

'I'm trying to help here you know, and yes, I do have some ideas about how you could market and develop the business, but you and I both know I'm not the solution. I'm only here until October and then I go back to uni, so what use would I be then? What you need is a proper partner in the business who can help you longer term. Jude might be busy, but surely he'd see the value in what you're doing? He'd be proud, wouldn't he? He'd want to help?'

Willow bit her lip. 'I know you're right. But I also know that Jude is a stickler for detail and he never goes after anything if it doesn't feel right, if the numbers don't stack up. I have to present this whole thing as a viable business, up and running, with a business plan, forecasts, and projections if he's ever going to take any notice of it. Otherwise he'll discount it out of hand.'

'Okay, I get that, but what's the problem; you'll have all that soon.'

Peter stared at her, waiting for a reply, watching while she took a calming breath.

'I trust you and I need your help, Peter, but if I tell you why I can't say anything to Jude at the moment, you have to promise me you won't repeat it. I haven't told a soul about this, not properly anyway.'

His normally pale complexion coloured quickly. 'Willow, how can I possibly do that when I don't know what it is you're going to say? It could put me in an untenable position.'

'I know, and I shouldn't ask, but I need your help.' She raised her hands in a helpless gesture. 'There's nothing more I can say. Once you know and understand why I feel the way I do, you can't unknow it. It has to be your decision. I'm not going to try to convince you.'

Peter had never been in such a position before. Sure he'd had friends tell him secrets, who hadn't, but this was different. From what he could see, Willow and Jude had a happy marriage, but if there was something that Willow felt she needed to keep secret from her husband, then it must be important. The other night while he'd waited with Jude for news about Beth, he had heard Jude's soft words about his wife, affectionate words, caring words; a loving inflection in his voice that could never be faked. He wasn't sure he wanted to hear anything that might call that into question.

Willow had said she wouldn't try to persuade him and, as he looked at her downcast face, he realised that unwittingly perhaps he had led them to this point. He couldn't blame her now for trying to explain when that was what he had asked her to do. He liked Willow. He loved her business and the way she lived her life, and now she was asking for his help.

'Go on,' he said slowly. 'What is it you need to say?'

She gave a nervous smile. 'You're going to think I'm an absolute nutter, but to be fair you wouldn't be the first . . . ' She took another deep breath. 'I see things sometimes . . . or feel things. Things which I know other people don't see or feel, but which give me a particular insight into a situation that's happening now . . . or in the future.' She glanced out of the window as if drawing strength from the view. 'Have you ever walked down our lane in the other direction, up towards Fallowfield?' she asked. 'The house just past the huge horse chestnut?'

'Only once or twice, although I'm not sure I really took much notice of it.'

'Middleton Estates own it. We have a tenant living there: Henry, and although you can't see it from the road, on the other side of the clearing is Jude's office.

Just past that is a five-bar gate that leads onto a track through the trees, at the other end of which are fields as far as you can see.'

'Which the company also owns?'

Willow nodded. 'I had a dream the other week that it was all gone. All the fields, the grasses, the hedges, torn up and replaced with row upon row of houses. Huge jagged craters left in the mud like an open wound.' She gave an involuntary shudder. 'Peter, it terrified me to see all of that meadow-land gone, ripped aside through greed, houses crushed together . . .'

Peter reached out a tentative hand to touch her arm in comfort.

'I know that's what Jude is planning. He's going to sell the land to some developer and build houses on it. I can't begin to imagine how much money it will make him . . . but however much it is, it will never be enough for his father. Andrew only ever taught Jude fear. Fear of being poor, fear of being despised by others, richer and more powerful than him, and all Jude ever wanted from his father was to be loved. But there isn't enough money in the world to make him love Jude, not properly, not like a father should: unconditionally, wholeheartedly. But Jude hasn't figured this out yet,' she said bitterly. 'His father will be behind this somewhere, egging him on, justifying his actions. Telling him you're only as good as your next million.' A tear dripped down her cheek. 'I can't let Jude do this to himself. I have to make him see that he has a life here, a good life, with people who love him for who he is. I have to show him that enough really can be enough.'

This wasn't what Peter had expected to hear from Willow, but curiously, it made sense. Now that Willow had said it out loud he could see the desire in Jude, the mercenary streak that ran through his veins, the way he dressed, the way he spoke sometimes. Jude was a person who liked life with a gilt edge. Peter fished in his pocket for a hanky, passing it to Willow and feeling his own emotions welling up. Willow wasn't like that. Whatever she had would be enough, and she'd give you her last bean if you asked for it. She wanted a successful business, but it wasn't money that motivated her, it was love. Love for anything that lived, breathed, or grew, but especially, love for Jude.

'Will he take your strawberry fields as well?' he asked gently.

Willow looked up sharply, her nose still buried in Peter's hanky. ' . . . I don't think so,' she replied, and then stronger, 'no, I'm sure he wouldn't do that . . . not to start with anyway, but it will come in time. What's to stop the developer wanting more and more?'

Peter thought quickly. 'So, assuming what you've said is true, your idea is to give Jude a viable alternative to his plan so that he doesn't sell the land. A business which ultimately you would run together, and one which he can see has a chance of being a success? He would stand to lose a huge amount of money, though, Willow. Do you really think it might work?'

She wiped her nose again. 'I don't know,' she whispered. 'But it's the only chance I've got.'

'You're going to have to speak to him about all this some time; you do know that, don't you? You might have got it all wrong, and—'

Willow shook her head urgently. 'I know, but not yet. I need to get things sorted out, Peter, I haven't got much time. I don't know how far advanced his plans are, or how much time I have on my side. It could only be a matter of weeks and, if I show my ideas to Jude now, without any of the assurances I know he'll look for, then I might as well not bother. I need something solid to divert his course of action, not a half-baked plan that would simply reinforce the notion that his own pursuits are the only realistic option for our future. I either need more time, or more results, and that's all there is to it.'

There was no knowing what amount of time they had, Peter could see that.

All this still might be for nothing, but they had to try, surely?

'Have you got a pen and a notebook I can scribble in? I need to know exactly what you've done so far.'

9

Jude turned his car into the secluded parking area with a flourish, covering the small distance to the guest parking spaces far more quickly than was necessary. His powerful car swung around, coming to a halt immediately beneath a security camera, one of several that ringed the car park. It didn't matter whether you were inside the building or outside, appearances were what mattered.

He levered his long legs out of the car, and reached into the back for his jacket. His Ralph Lauren suit clung in all the right places, the jacket settling effortlessly along his shoulders, the crisp shirt he'd chosen, just a little tighter than he would normally wear. He'd debated buying a new suit for the occasion but decided that this would deliver the wrong message. He didn't want to look as though he was trying to impress; he simply wanted to be impressive, and far better to arrive wearing an old favourite that showed how accustomed he was to fine clothes than to look like some jumped-up barrow boy. He straightened his cufflinks and closed the car door with a clunk.

The cameras tracked him silently as he walked. He wouldn't need to announce his arrival. By the time he pushed open the door into the elegant glass atrium, Emily would have alerted her boss to his presence and would rise to greet him, enquiring politely about his journey and escorting him personally up to the third floor. The board room would already be set up, and her order for fresh coffee would take only a matter of seconds as he approached the building. Edward would be ready for him, as, no doubt, would Olivia. He only hoped he was ready for them.

His face had held a gracious smile for the whole distance across the car park to the reception area, and only now, as he reached out a hand for the door, did he allow himself to clench his jaws together momentarily. By the time he met Emily's outstretched hand, the smile was back. The next hour would possibly be the most important of his career, and he pushed the memory of the last conversation with his father away, thrusting it deep into a place where, today at least, it would not surface. He concentrated on Emily's face, not only on what she was saying, but what her eyes told him too. Secretaries always knew what was going down, and he'd never met one yet who'd been able to hide it.

Olivia met him as he stepped from the lift, her brown eyes twinkling mischievously. She was wearing a bright red dress, clingy and low cut, and Jude let his eyes wander its length for just a moment longer than casual interest might dictate. He met her gaze with a smile, leaning in for the customary kiss on both cheeks.

Her cheek was soft against his, as she pressed her body up against him, one hand lingering against his arm as she slowly stroked its length. When she finally pulled away, her eyes flashed like a cat in the night, and Jude let a soft sigh whisper into the space between them.

'Jude, you're looking even more ravishing than the last time we met. How will I ever keep my hands off you?'

He placed a hand in the small of her back as she turned around, applying just enough pressure to the base of her spine. His other hand was already extended towards her husband who he had spied walking soundlessly across the deep carpet to join them.

'Edward, a pleasure as always,' he smiled.

The hand that shook his was cool despite the warmth of the day.

'Jude,' he nodded in return, and then taking his wife's arm, 'Shall we?' He motioned towards the board room.

Inside, the table which would easily accommodate twelve was laid for just the three of them. A black jotter marked each place, a white coffee cup at its top right-hand corner. Apart from the carafe of fresh coffee, the table held a marble platter with milk, sugar, and a plate filled with a dozen or so small pastries. The only other thing on the table was a sheaf of thick white paper.

As Jude sat in the space indicated, Emily materialised back into the room, holding a trio of iPads, one of which she set up on the table in front of him. The others she passed to Edward and Olivia before soundlessly leaving the room. It was like a dance, a bizarre mating ritual, but Jude knew the moves, and he played them effortlessly.

The door closed behind them with a soft click as he waited for Edward to speak. His heart was pounding.

'Well then, Jude, how about it?' He grinned. 'Is today a good day to make an obscene amount of money?'

'It's always a good day for making money, Eddie, but obscenity can sometimes take a little longer.' He flashed a candid smile. 'And I never sign anything on an empty stomach. May I?' he asked, indicating the tray of pastries.

Olivia slipped out of her seat and began to pour the coffee. 'Help yourself,' she purred. The pastries were not the only thing being offered on a plate.

'I've taken the liberty of summarising the key points of our agreement,' said Edward, 'which you can find in front of you, although you and I both know we could recite them in our sleep. I want to be sure that you're happy with everything, Jude. It's important to me that there are no doubts from your perspective; Jennings Pemberton has built its reputation on integrity and, important though this deal is, for both of us, I've no wish to jeopardise what we've worked so hard for on a detail overlooked, or a technicality. Please take all the time you need before signing.'

Jude smiled. Edward was smooth, there was no denying it, but the fact of the matter was that Jude would not be sitting here today if he were in any way unsure about the deal on the table. Jude paid his lawyers a great deal of money to make sure that every detail was locked down, and indeed Jude himself had set the terms of this deal. There was never going to be any deviation from its specifications, he simply would not allow it. Today had been a very long time coming, and Jennings Pemberton were certainly not the first organisation with whom he had sought to broker a deal. It was gracious of Edward to make it appear that they were doing him a favour, but really it couldn't be farther from the truth. Even the parcel of land he'd thrown in as a sweetener had been chosen with the utmost care. Completely disingenuous on his part of course; he was well aware that there was every possibility that planning permission would be granted on it, but it didn't hurt to feign ignorance. Punters liked to think they were getting one over on the seller, and for all his integrity, Edward was no different.

He sipped his coffee, savouring the rich taste. 'I'm happy to sign, Eddie,' he said. 'I trust you received Andrew's instructions yesterday?'

'On the dotted line, Jude, all present and correct.'

Jude lifted the cup to his lips once

more, letting it hide the outward breath he released. Andrew's co-operation had been by no means assured, and after their argument of the other evening there was a small, but none the less, significant risk that he would veto the agreement at the last minute. Jude was mightily relieved to see that Andrew's mercenary tendencies still held. Cold-hearted he might be, but he was no fool, and given the choice of either signing and accepting the new arrangements or losing a good deal of virtually free money, was there really any other choice open to him?

Edward reached inside his jacket pocket to retrieve a midnight blue fountain pen that exactly matched the colour of his tie, and slid it along the table towards Jude.

Jude looked down at the sheaf of paper on the blotter in front of him. He scanned the pages with a practised eye, and flipped to the last page with a casual flick of his wrist. He signed his name on the bottom without a second glance.

As if a spell had been broken, the

calculated atmosphere in the room relaxed, and jackets were removed, ties were loosened and the conversation flowed amiably. Olivia rubbed her foot along Jude's calf a total of three times and Jude enquired politely how their eldest daughter's GCSEs had gone. Forty-nine minutes after he first entered the building, Jude bid a cheerful good-bye to Emily in reception and walked back out to the car park. Moments later, he swung out past the security cameras with just the same panache as when he had entered.

He waited until he was several streets from the offices of Jennings Pemberton before pulling his car to the side of the road, opening his door and vomiting the two almond pastries and Olivia's unwelcome attention and cloying perfume into the cool grass of the verge.

10

It was difficult to see how Freya was managing to type anything on her laptop. It was precariously poised on a pile of papers, resting at such a slant that it bounced up and down each time she typed. Willow hovered in the doorway for a moment, unwilling to break Freya's concentration, but also fascinated to see her working in such a haphazard fashion. As she watched, Freya lifted up her laptop, peered at the piece of paper directly underneath it, and then carried on typing completely oblivious to how absurd she looked.

Sam leaned towards Willow. 'She's been like that for hours. Every time I come in, the paper level has risen another inch. God knows where it's all coming from. In fact, if you hadn't arrived, I'd be worried I might lose her altogether.'

'I can hear you, you know,' came the disembodied voice from behind the laptop. 'Sorry, Willow, I'll be with you in a minute . . . I just want to finish this sentence . . . while it's all in my head.'

'I'll put the kettle on.' Sam grinned, crossing the room.

Willow looked around her at the homely kitchen. When they were children, she used to come here at least once a week after netball practice. Freya's dad would make them hot chocolate and they would sit and giggle their way through copies of *Just Seventeen*. She'd never dreamed that years later they would still be here, hatching plans and schemes of a different kind. But it felt right; the happy energy in the room was still here after all this time, as if nothing had changed, and even Freya herself didn't look much different to how she had then, frantically trying to finish her homework before school the next day. When Freya's father had died last year, it had looked for a while as if she might lose both the farm and her childhood home, but today, with Sam at her side, their future was secure. She could only hope that her own plans would bring about a similar resolution for her and Jude.

Freya's dark head bobbed up from behind the screen, and she laid the laptop to one side.

'Sorry about that, but I've been trying to nail this particular paragraph all morning, and the perfect words suddenly came to me.' She got up from the table and gave Willow a hug. 'I'm like a thing possessed, but then I guess you feel that way too,' she added.

Willow smiled at Sam as he handed her a cup of tea. 'There never seem to be enough hours in the day. Everything I do spawns more and more jobs . . . I've never been so excited, though. I can't stop thinking about stuff, and even though things are getting done, I've a horrible feeling I'm getting carried away.'

Freya nodded repeatedly. 'Oh yeah,' she said. 'Been there, done that . . . still there in fact.' She laughed. 'Look, I'll show you.'

She took Willow's arm, just as Sam butted in. 'I'm going to leave you two for a bit and take my tea somewhere a little more peaceful, but I'll come back and check on you in about half an hour, Willow, just to make sure you're still with us. If you need me to come and rescue you before then, just shout, okay?' He winked at Freya. 'Go easy on her . . . and remember to breathe.'

Freya picked up her pencil preparing to throw it as Sam ducked out of the room. 'Cheeky sod, he's just as excited as I am.'

'So what are you up to now?' asked Willow, sitting down and peering at the assortment of leaflets and brochures on the table.

Freya turned the laptop screen around to face her friend.

'The Appleyard Community Juice Pressing Scheme,' she announced proudly. 'We're not short of a few fruit trees here in Herefordshire as you know, and it suddenly struck me what a wonderful resource we have. There are loads of people around here who'd like to make their own juice but haven't got the right equipment. Even a single tree in your garden is enough – one bucket load of apples could make about five bottles of juice, and we'll pasteurise it too, so it will last for about a year.'

Willow looked at the vibrant images on the screen. She scratched the side of her nose. 'But don't you want people to buy the juice you make?'

'Of course.' Freya grinned. 'But this way we get the best of both worlds. We'll make and sell our own juice products, with a little help from you of course, and by aiming these products at carefully selected retailers, we won't be saturating the market locally which will give the range more of a specialty feel to it. People will still have to pay for the pressing service, so that will generate additional income, keep our machines running and, with any luck, score us some brownie points with the local community, especially if we stress the fundraising possibilities for groups who want to press juice for a profit themselves.' She looked down fondly at the screen. 'It might also result in even more sales, perversely. Just suppose you press your own juice, proudly take home your bottles and then drink them over the course of the next few weeks. Where are you going to get more from, now that you've developed a taste for the fresh stuff?'

'Ah . . . clever,' said Willow. 'You know that actually makes sense. What a brilliant idea.'

'I know,' replied Freya, beaming. 'I'm a genius. Seriously though, it does make sound business sense, but I like the whole idea of the community thing too. I feel like I've been given a second chance with Appleyard, and I'd like to keep that luck running if I can.'

Willow looked down at the table again. 'And this is research, is it?'

'Mainly,' replied Freya. 'Information from other companies offering a similar service, but I've also got brochures here giving all the technical specifications for our equipment as well. We might be asked all sorts of questions by prospective users of the scheme, and I don't want to be caught napping. We could need to be pressing as early as August, and that doesn't give us much time to get all our marketing information out there and be ready for business.'

'So you need to know where I am with Willowberries?'

Freya nodded. 'I just love that name.' She sighed. 'We make such a perfect combination, don't we? Appleyard Juices and Willowberries nectar, it's almost as if it was meant to be — I mean who wouldn't want to buy us?'

Willow fished in the bag she had brought with her, carefully pulling out a cardboard box and laying it on the table in front of her. Wrapped around it was a vibrantly printed sleeve of cardboard the exact colour of a dusky Victoria plum. A froth of white elderflowers trailed across one corner, curling around the lettering that formed the company name. She looked at Freya's astonished face.

'Go on, open it,' she said.

Freya moved her laptop further to one side and slid the box towards her.

'I daren't, it's too beautiful,' she replied, running her fingers across the surface. 'Is this one of the sample boxes that you were talking about?'

Willow's smile was wide. 'They turned out better than I could ever have hoped. They were Peter's idea, but Henry did all the design work of course, and his girlfriend gave me the name of the people she uses for packaging.'

'And Merry has sent these out to the list of folk that she knows?'

'Some of them, yes, about twenty in all to start with. It was a pretty long list, but we picked some retailers, some hotels and a couple of restaurants too. All people she's dealt with before and recommends. Fingers crossed we get one or two bites.'

Freya looked down at the box in front of her. 'I'd eat *this*.' She grinned. 'It looks good enough.'

Carefully, she removed the sleeve from the outside, and levered open the lid of the box. A subtle waft of summery fragrance rose up. She inhaled happily.

'Mmm, what's this?' she queried.

'Elderflower oil, dabbed onto the bottom of the box. I thought it would help to appeal to all the senses,' said Willow.

'Oh God, I'm fairly drooling . . . '

She lifted out a small bottle from the box, a lime green label swinging from its neck. *Drink Me* it read.

I am elderflowers, gathered when the sun warms the blooms and bees dance in the hedgerows.
I am steeped with sugar and juicy Sicilian lemons.
I am Willowberries Elderflower Nectar.

Next a tiny jar emerged with a label bearing the instruction *Eat Me*.

I am fat strawberries that dribble down your chin, gathered from a field where skylarks sing.
I've begged a little lemon juice, sugar, and elderflower cordial to keep me company.
I am Willowberries Strawberry and Elderflower Preserve.

Freya set this gently to one side, bringing out the last of the tiny containers, this time a small pot with a vibrant plum label. *Imagine me*, it read.

I am gooseberries, golden orbs bursting in the morning sun.
I am singing with sugar and elderflower cordial and whipped into soft velvety peaks of double cream.
I am Willowberries Gooseberry and Elderflower Cream Ice.

She sat back in her chair, for a moment totally lost for words. Willow was studying her, trying to read her expression.

'The labels are just a little bit of folly,' supplied Willow. 'I thought they might add to the sense of magic; you know like Alice in Wonderland . . .'

'Willow, these are inspired! I've never seen anything like this, but what a fantastic idea, it works beautifully.'

'There's some literature in there as well, giving details of the available flavours, ingredients, as well as how they're made. I've tasted so many cordials and eaten so much ice cream this week I'll be the size of a house soon, but fortunately for my waistline, this is the final list, well for the time being anyway. We've settled on eight flavours of ice cream to start with and six different cordials, together with nine types of preserves and curds.'

It had taken Willow quite some time to decide which of her favourite recipes to concentrate on, but she knew that if they were to have any chance of success she had to keep things simple. The number of flavours was sensible, and as they were seasonal, it would give them the opportunity to concentrate on each, one at a time, until they were really up and running. They were a mixture of the traditional and the more exotic, a little risky potentially, but Willow wanted to provide not just the familiar, but the enticing too. Her lemon and rose geranium cordial might sound unusual, but she'd buy a bottle just for the colour alone.

'These sound amazing.' Freya grinned,

looking at the stylish literature. 'I can't wait to try them.'

'Well, some of the flavours I can get to you straight away, but the rosehips for example won't be available until the autumn. You'll just have to take my word for how gorgeous it is.'

'The main thing is that I get an idea of what you're going to produce. There will be plenty of time for us to experiment with our fruit juice blends later in the year. We won't be harvesting for months yet, but that's the beauty of it. It will give you time to start producing, and we'll be busy juicing other people's fruit until our own are ready to harvest.'

'I'm going to see Merry later to take her some more literature too, so she can help promote Willowberries through the shop. I'd like her opinion on a few other things as well; she knows so much about merchandising.'

Freya sucked in a quick breath. 'Did she tell you she's got someone coming to see her from *Country Living*? How amazing is that?'

Willow stared at her. 'What, *the* Country Living? As in the magazine? How on earth did she manage that?'

'Sheer fluke I think. A reporter did a piece on the shop for the local paper, talking about the artist who owned it before and how Merry has breathed new life into it by paying homage to him. Someone from the magazine spotted the article whilst they were staying with some relative or another for a wedding down here. I haven't got the whole story. They only called yesterday, and Merry was a tad excited when she told me.' She grinned at Willow. 'I could hardly understand a word she was saying . . .'

'I bet.' She laughed. 'What wonderful publicity for her, though, and such a stroke of luck.'

'Merry seemed to think that Christopher himself might have had something to do with it.' Freya winked. 'I did point out that he'd been dead for a couple of years, but that didn't seem to deter her.'

'Maybe she's found her guardian angel,' replied Willow. 'Stranger things have happened.' She thought back to the bleak time in Freya's life just after her father died and the transformation that had been brought about by her dark, curly-haired stranger.

Freya nodded, clearly understanding her meaning. 'Stranger things indeed,' she said. 'So who's your guardian angel then, Willow?'

A worried frown crossed Willow's face. 'I'd like to say maybe my grandma Gilly, but I'm not sure there's anyone watching over me right now,' she said seriously. 'I'm running out of time, so if they're out there, it would be nice if they could make their presence felt a bit sharpish.'

'Are you still having those dreams?' asked Freya, a concerned note to her voice.

Willow nodded. 'More and more. Always the same. And Jude is definitely up to something, he's like the proverbial cat on a hot tin roof, and he's working harder than ever. I've barely seen him.'

'Maybe you should talk to him, Willow.

Then at least you'd know where you are, and what you're up against.'

Willow shook her head violently this time. 'No. Not until I'm certain. Not until I'm ready with all of this. I have to prove to him that this could work for us.'

Willow closed her eyes momentarily. She was getting scared now. The dreams were getting stronger and stronger, still most often at night, but now during the day as well, with an intensity that made her feel quite sick. She had been washing up a couple of nights ago when Jude had come into the kitchen and slid his arms around her waist. The sudden shock of the images which had forced their way into her mind had nearly taken her legs from under her, and had Jude not been there to catch her, she would have fallen. It had taken all her powers of persuasion to convince him not to call a doctor, so how could she confide in him now? He'd think her ill, or worse, mad, and she would never be able to convince him that her fledgling business was worth pursuing.

She gave Freya a bright smile, knowing that she disproved of her silence as far as Jude was concerned. 'I'll have a chat to him soon; I'd like to get a few more things underway first, that's all, and then I'll hit him with my amazing ideas and business prowess. He won't be able to believe it.'

The look on Freya's face was far from convinced, but she returned Willow's smile anyway.

'Give my love to Merry, won't you,' she said, changing the subject. 'I can't wait to hear all the gossip about the magazine.'

'Merry will be going nuts, making sure every little detail is perfect, but she's been such a star helping me out, she deserves to have a massive success on her hands.'

'So do we all,' remarked Freya. 'Don't you think? It's been quite a year one way or another, and it's not over yet, not by a long chalk.'

11

'These are literally walking out of the door,' said Merry, standing back proudly to admire her display. 'I'd say a good part of the village is having strawberries with their tea tonight, and I can't say I blame them. Don't they look gorgeous . . . and the smell . . . ' She breathed in deeply.

Willow fanned her face. It was warm in the shop now that the afternoon sun was streaming through the door, but Merry was right, it brought out the smell of the ripe fruit beautifully.

'I've been telling everybody who comes in that we're going to be selling more of your produce soon, and so far, the reaction has been very positive. I think it might be the weather, but people's eyes light up when I mention ice cream or your cordials. You're definitely onto a winner there.'

She motioned for Willow to follow her through into the back room.

'I thought I could put the freezer here, and by moving this stand around, I can fit in some shelving next to it where I can display your full range in time. What do you think?' she asked. 'Of course they'll marry beautifully with Freya and Sam's juices come the autumn.'

Willow stared at the room around her, feeling quite overcome with emotion. 'I'm absolutely gobsmacked, Merry. I can't believe that you've done all this for me. It's perfect.' Her eyes were shining, but she made no move to wipe the tears away.

Merry clasped her hands. 'It's perfect for us too, you know. The shop needed something to make it stand out —' She caught sight of Willow's face and laughed. 'Yes, apart from the décor! We needed to find a niche in the market that would set us above being simply the village shop. I wanted this place to be something special, and you and Freya have provided the perfect start for us. I've spent the last few days touring the villages and towns locally, and I've found the most amazing suppliers, from cheeses, to wines and everything else in between, and all from small businesses within a twenty mile radius. I want to turn us into a gourmet food centre. We can offer the products online and do food demonstrations and —' She stopped suddenly. 'What's the matter, Willow? Are you okay?'

Willow was aware that her mouth had dropped open. She closed it, a huge grin immediately swamping her face as a tide of excitement swept over her. 'I don't suppose you need any extra space for these demonstrations . . . or courses even . . . '

Merry narrowed her eyes. 'Why, what are you thinking?' she asked.

'Only that Peter and I were chatting the other day, like you, trying to come up with something that might make us a bit different from the competition. Purely by chance, one of his friends gave us the most brilliant idea.'

'Go on,' said Merry, intrigued.

'I had a few of Peter's friends over for a day recently to help us pick elderflowers and gooseberries. One of them, a young girl, seemed quite nervous to start with, but as the day went on, forgive the pun, she really blossomed. I've just had a message from her to say thanks for giving her the opportunity to help out, and how much she had enjoyed the experience. It struck me that we could offer residential cookery courses or retreats, perhaps in exchange for help to make our products. We could incorporate all kinds of things so that people learn new skills or have a chance to brush up on old ones, and while we're doing that, we get a ready workforce. We've got that huge barn we could transform as time goes on, and if any of your suppliers would be willing to come and teach their skills as well, then —'

It was Merry's turn to have her mouth drop open. 'Oh, my God,' she said slowly. 'We have to make this work, Willow. *Country Living* are going to love this! They want to talk to me about what we've already done here, but also what plans we have in the future to develop the shop. They're very keen on the flourishing rural business angle. If we can come up with ways like this of linking all our businesses, it would be perfect.'

'When are they coming?' Willow breathed.

'Next Friday, a little over a week away. We've probably just got time to pull something together for them. It doesn't have to be concrete, but we would need to show how it might work, how we would set it up in principle, what resources we have, that kind of thing. Would that be possible, do you think, or are we just plain mad?'

Willow gave an excited squeal. 'Mad!' She laughed. 'Mad as March bloody hares, but we have to do this, Merry, we have to!'

★ ★ ★

The journey back into town passed in a blur of wild ideas, and Willow had parked the car before she realised that she couldn't even remember turning into the High Street. She was desperate to get back home and speak to Peter, but she needed to stop and get some extra cash out for him. It was payday at the end of the week, but he had put in so many extra hours of late that a little bonus was the least she could do.

Willow snatched up her bag from the passenger side and was only about fifty metres or so from the bank when she realised that Jude was standing on the pavement outside, and he wasn't alone. He shook Henry's hand, his left arm reaching out to grip his shoulder in the classic configuration of a deal just sealed. She would have waved, had her ears not been filled with a sudden roaring, and for a moment she was completely disorientated.

Somehow, she made it back to the car, where she sat for a little while, shaking, before starting the engine and drawing away as slowly as she could. She needed time to think and had no desire to be seen by anyone she knew, least of all her husband. She drove at a snail's pace along the back road and eventually stopped the car just over the bridge into their village, throwing open the door and drawing in lungs full of fresh air.

She breathed deeply for a few minutes, trying to calm the voices in her head. Voices that mocked and derided her. How could she have been so stupid, so complacent? So very wrong.

After a few minutes, she drove off again, more purposeful this time, heat gathering at the back of her neck, and a burning anger swelling inside her. In the past, her dreams had been little more than pointers, a heightened sense of intuition perhaps, but always clear in their meaning. They had never sought to mislead her or caused her any real anxiety, but these past few weeks had been so different. The visions had been vivid, powerful even, consuming her senses for several minutes at a time, and in the last couple of days not confined to night-time either, when her perception was surely at its greatest. But still she had missed something, perhaps the most

161

vital thing of all. She had seen a glimpse into a future, of that she was sure, but until today, she had mistakenly believed Andrew to be at the root of it all. It had never crossed her mind that it might be someone else . . . She needed to see more, had to know if what she'd seen today was the truth, and there was only one place she could do it: by the very fields that were the source of her vision.

The driveway was empty as she turned up to the house, and she abandoned the car at an angle, keys still in the ignition. In a matter of minutes, she had reached her destination and she stood in front of the five-bar gate that lead onto the track and the open land beyond.

It was here that she had first seen the horrific sight of their fields torn asunder to make way for row upon row of houses. The meadow-land with its wild flowers and grasses, home to so many, all gone; ripped away to make homes of a different kind. She put her hands on the gate, dropped her head and closed her eyes.

She had expected the vision to come

to her straight away. Sometimes at night now it clamoured for her attention so much she had to fight to push it away, but now all she felt was a deep and languid peace, quite the opposite from what she had been expecting. It confused her even more. Here, in the very place she had seen in her dream, the images should be stronger than ever, but even as she sought to empty her mind of chatter all she could see were the tall heads of the grasses gently swaying in the breeze, livestock nibbling at the fresh green shoots of spring and the march hares leaping in their ritual dance. There was nothing of the carnage that had filled her head so recently. She felt her breathing begin to ease until all that filled her head was the rushing of the wind in the trees.

A light touch on her arm made her jump.

'Willow?'

She opened her eyes to find Delilah looking at her anxiously, her voice gentle. She had the feeling it wasn't the first time she had spoken to her. The two dogs milled around her as she stood, a nervous smile on her face.

'Are you okay?' Delilah asked. 'You look like you're away with the faeries.'

Willow swallowed hard, looking backwards and forwards between the gate and the face in front of her. Maybe Delilah was right. Maybe that's exactly where she was. In the land of the faeries, being deluded by visions and a certainty that what they showed her was the truth. Too busy chasing dreams instead of dealing with the reality that was under her nose. And now she was more confused than ever. She had believed that what she was trying to achieve was the right thing for her and her family, for the way in which they lived their lives. To help Jude turn away from a downward spiral into money-grabbing materialism, towards living a simpler, more nurturing and sustainable way of life. In doing so, she had reached out for help to someone she had thought to be a friend. She never imagined for one minute that Henry would be the one to betray her.

Warm fur brushed against Willow's legs and she became aware of Delilah's anxious face still studying her. She needed to be anywhere but here.

'Sorry,' she started. 'I came over a bit faint there for a minute. I'm okay now, though.'

Delilah regarded her suspiciously. 'Are you sure, 'cause you still look a bit peaky to me.'

Willow waved an airy hand. 'Honestly, I'll be fine. I didn't have much for lunch, and I think the heat got to me a bit.'

'You could come inside and have some water,' added Delilah. 'Sit down for a minute.'

The dogs were still milling aimlessly.

'No, don't worry. You go and enjoy your walk. I'll just wander home and have a glass of something cool.' She smiled as reassuringly as she could, beginning to back away down the lane. 'I'll catch you later,' she added. 'I haven't forgotten about my offer of dinner. We should fix something up.' She gave the dogs a final pat and turned away.

★ ★ ★

Delilah watched her walk a little way before turning in the other direction. She pulled her mobile from the pocket of her shorts and dialled Henry's number. He answered almost straight away.

'Are you still with Jude?' she asked urgently.

'No, I've just left, why?'

'It's almost as if Willow knows,' whispered Delilah, 'but I thought Jude wasn't going to say anything to her just yet. Has he changed his mind?'

'No,' replied Henry. 'The only people that know are us and Jude, I'm sure of it. Beside there's no way Jude would say anything until the deal goes through, he wants it to be a surprise.'

There was silence on the line for a moment.

'Is everything all right?' Henry prompted.

'I don't know . . . it's weird. I've just met Willow in the lane by the gate. She was staring right at the fields, and the look on her face was . . . I dunno, but she didn't look happy. She gave me some story about feeling faint, but she didn't want any help.'

'That does seem a bit odd,' agreed Henry. 'Jude is sure she'll be over the moon when she finds out . . . are you still okay, though?'

Delilah couldn't help herself and gave an excited skip. 'Lover, I'm blinkin' ecstatic!' she gushed.

She could hear Henry's smile as he replied. 'Well, then, we'll just have to wait and see. And that won't be long; Jude said he could get the call from his bank as early as tomorrow. I'm still sure Willow doesn't know anything about it, and when she does find out, I'm pretty certain she'll be as excited as we are. Perhaps it's like she said, and she just felt hot, that's all.'

'I'm sure you're right,' answered Delilah. 'After all, it can't really be anything else, can it?'

12

It felt to Willow as if she had been sitting in the same spot since yesterday. There seemed little point in doing much else.

The door to her potions room as Peter had once called it, remained firmly closed. She had gone in there early this morning to retrieve grandma Gilly's notebook, but apart from that she had no intention of stepping inside. The last batch of elderflowers would wither and turn brown during the day if they were left unprocessed, but Willow didn't care if they were unusable. It seemed fitting somehow that the fragrant frothy white heads would lose their strength and wither and die. It was much how she felt herself.

Jude had been his usual loving and attentive self last night, playing with the girls after tea, a quiet game, mindful of Beth's arm which was still quite sore. He had them in fits of giggles as he read their bedtime story with his repertoire of silly voices which they loved. It had been easy to pretend that everything was fine during the early evening when there were things to be done and Willow could keep busy but, as soon as the girls were in bed, he had come straight to her side. She looked tired he had said, working too hard, and had offered to run her a soothing bath. Willow had never known Jude to behave in any other way, but now she caught herself watching him, questioning his motives. Was it attentiveness, or guilt at his betrayal? Keeping her sweet until the time when he would have to tell her what he had done.

Eventually, after she feigned a migraine and her replies became ever more monosyllabic with each question, Jude had left her to the quiet solitude she had wished for. He had slept curled around her back though, just as he always did, but instead of welcoming the warmth and comfort his arms provided like she would normally do, he had felt heavy, and confining, pinning her to the bed, and she longed for some space to think and to breathe. She hated the way it made her feel.

This morning her tiredness had been real, her face pale and drawn, and even though Jude needed to get to his office early, he promised to look in on her at lunchtime. It was now nearly eleven o'clock, and she had not moved for some time. Another message from Merry flashed up on the screen of her mobile, at least the fifth since yesterday. She picked up her phone to tap out a reply.

Hi, sorry not to reply earlier, but Amy is really poorly bless her, and I can't leave her today. I'll ring you later, so we can fix up when to meet, hope that's okay? Still madly excited! Xx

Pressing send, she tossed her phone back onto the table with a sigh. She had bought herself time with her lies, that was all, but some time fairly soon she would have to make a decision. In all the years she had been married to Jude, they had never even argued, and she certainly had never had cause to doubt their relationship, it was simply not on her radar. Now though, with one fell swoop, everything she believed about their life together had been called into question. It wasn't only Jude's duplicity that she was struggling to deal with, but her own, for wasn't she just as bad? She had kept secrets too, convincing herself that what she was doing was right without even discussing it with Jude, not once. In all honesty, Jude probably thought he was doing the right thing for his family, just as she did herself, so which of them was right? They were both as bad as one another, she thought bitterly.

She'd been such a fool to think that her stupid business venture would be the thing to make the difference to their lives. So blinded was she by her ego and fanciful dreams that she had forgotten how to share, to talk, and to love. She could never agree with what Jude had done, but how would he feel when he found out how she had been planning to ambush his plans too. To discount them out of hand by thrusting her own, better idea under his nose. She loved Jude so much, always had, and a life without him was unthinkable, but for the first time in her marriage she was worried for their future. A single tear, the first she had shed, made its way down her cheek, and as it dripped from the end of her chin, a bout of crying gripped her so fiercely she could scarcely breathe. She lowered her head to the table and howled like a wounded animal.

Some time later she awoke, much to her surprise, to find she was lying beneath the cool sheets of her bed. She vaguely remembered Jude talking to her, when she was still slumped at the table. The tears had dried up by then, but she was listless and unresponsive, and he had led her to bed without protest. He had brought cool flannels for her forehead and sweet drinks in the dimmed room, and then left her to the effortless escape of sleep.

She lifted her head weakly to look

at the clock beside her bed, astonished to discover it was early evening. Panic lurched in her stomach at the thought of the girls worried and alone after school, but a burble of laughter reached her from along the hallway, and she realised that they were having their evening bath. It had always been the same, she remembered. Any time she had been unwell, or simply exhausted with the twins' demands when they were tiny, Jude had been there, without a second thought, caring for the girls, and for her. He worked so hard himself and yet any free time he had, he devoted to them, never to himself. He'd been the best father and the best husband she could wish for. A lump rose in her throat.

A cool breeze ruffled the curtains at the window, and she let the air play over her skin. She closed her eyes again, pressing her head deeper into the pillow. She would have to deal with all of this soon, she knew that, but not today. She was so tired and all she craved now was to be released from pain. She slept.

There was no lightning this time to illuminate the scene, no pouring rain, but instead a blazing sun shone down, bouncing off the stark pale streets intersected by rows and rows of houses. Tired gardens drooped in the heat and a haze shimmered from the cars as they passed. A young mother wheeled a pushchair, sweat collecting on her back as she bent to the child inside who was hot and fretful. There was no shade anywhere.

And then she saw it. The huge oak tree that had always guarded the entrance to the fields. A tree under which she had played with the girls, collecting wildflowers, having tea parties with their dolls, making daisy chains and lying on their backs staring up at the sky, making shapes from the clouds that floated past. The same tree was now fenced off, contained, unreachable, and undesirable. Willow woke, heart pounding, her own sweat gluing her nightdress to her body. The vision was just as clear as before and she tried to slow her breathing.

As her eyes adjusted to the darkness in the room, she became aware of movement beside her, and ragged breathing that was not her own. A sliver of moonlight lay across Jude's body and without thinking Willow slipped her hand into its light, feeling the comfort it brought. She crept soundlessly from the bed and pulled back the curtains, letting the silvery rays flood the room. It was a full moon; how could she have forgotten?

She climbed back into bed, moving closer to Jude, seeing the sheen of perspiration on his face as he dreamed. His eyelids fluttered, his mouth parted as he fought against the images in his mind. His fingers opened and closed on the sheet beside her, seeking solace, seeking comfort from her, and as she slid her fingers into his, she gasped as his terror filled her too.

Willow stared at her husband, a man she had loved for most of her life, and for the second time that day wondered how she had been so foolish, how she could have got it so completely wrong? Her dreams had plagued her for weeks, visions that were so real, they had haunted her, waking in her a terror of what they could mean; but as she looked at Jude's face, struggling and in pain, she realised that the fear had never been hers to begin with, and neither were the dreams. They were Jude's.

13

A missing PE kit had cut a huge swathe through Willow's available time this morning, and she barely had time to talk to Jude beyond vehement assurances that she was now fine and that he was not to worry about her. He rushed out of the house as soon as he could, claiming he needed an early start.

They had slept entwined together, just like they had in the early days of their relationship when they could scarcely bear to be apart for more than a few minutes. Jude's breathing had eased in time during the night as his dream passed, and Willow held him close, stroking his cheek and gazing at the face of the man too scared to share his fears with her for dread of seeming weak, a failure in her eyes, just like he had been in his father's his whole life. All he had ever wanted was to be loved, and although hate was not an emotion that Willow agreed with, in that moment she had never loathed Andrew more.

She knew now that the business deal that Jude was on the verge of was not one to sell their land, but somehow to save it. She had no idea why or how this had come about, or indeed where Henry came into it, but, given the urgency she now sensed in Jude, she realised the axe was about to fall one way or another. Whatever happened, Willow would not let another day pass without speaking to Jude and discovering the truth. Yesterday, she had convinced herself that her fledgling business was sheer folly, an exercise in flattering her ego and nothing more, but now she wondered whether her original thoughts had been right; that Willowberries might possibly be a viable alternative for their future.

The room at the end of the hallway beckoned to her once more and, scooping up a pile of letters from the doormat, she slowly walked its length, savouring the moment before she pushed open the door and breathed in the sweet smell of summer. Once inside she tossed the letters onto the table and smiled broadly as if greeting an old friend. It was time to get down to business.

One of the first things she needed to do was find Peter. She had shamefully left him to his own devices over the last day or so, and she couldn't blame him for keeping out of her way. Yesterday, she had told him she had a migraine and, whether or not he believed her, she had probably been quite short with him. He hadn't appeared at all yet this morning. She had an apology to make, but she also needed to ask him something very important. She gathered up the crate of elderflowers that had indeed withered the day before and carried them out of the back door. Dead things had no place inside a house for the living. This afternoon she would replace them, and another batch of cordial would be underway.

She collected a stray mug from the table and picked up the letters again, scanning the envelopes for anything more exciting than the electricity bill. She was still staring open-mouthed in shock at the letter in her hand when Jude came flying through the back door, her shouted name on his lips.

There was a moment's hesitation as he grinned at her before scooping her up and whirling her around. A stray splash of coffee flew from the cup and splattered against the wall, but neither of them saw it.

'Oh God, Willow, I've done it!' shouted Jude. 'I'm finally free . . . we're free!' he bellowed, too excited to restrain himself. He set her down momentarily before grinning like a loon and picking her up once more. He buried his face in the side of her neck, kissing her over and over.

Willow giggled. 'Put me down,' she managed through her laughter, struggling to hold onto the things in her hands. 'What on earth has got into you? The last time I saw you this excited . . . well, I can't actually remember ever seeing you this excited before.'

He did as she asked, stepping away

slightly to look at her better. His chest was heaving, his eyes shining, and yet bizarrely he looked calmer and more relaxed than she had seen him in weeks.

'Do you want to come and sit down and tell me what it is that's got you so worked up? I don't think I can stand the suspense.'

Jude raked a hand through his hair. 'Yes . . . no . . . I don't think I can. I don't think I can sit still for that long.'

Willow put her hands on her hips and gave him her best 'I'm standing no nonsense' stare. 'I'll superglue your trousers to the chair if I have to.'

Willow's heart was pounding too, she realised, but her own news would have to wait a while. Whatever Jude was trying to tell her must surely be connected with the source of their dreams. She had a feeling she might remember this moment for some time to come.

She sat at the table and waited for him to join her, watching his face expectantly, but his expression hardly changed. He looked overjoyed, and

181

excited, but something else glittered in his eyes, and as his gaze met hers, she understood what it was. He looked jubilant.

'I don't really know where to start,' he began, 'and I know I probably should have discussed this with you before, but when I tell you I hope you'll understand why I didn't.' He paused for a moment to gather his thoughts. 'It's complicated, but maybe I should start at the end and work backwards.'

Willow nodded encouragement as Jude took a deep breath.

'I've sold the business,' he said, laying down the sentence in the room like an unexploded bomb. 'I no longer have any share in Middleton Estates,' he added as if his previous statement wasn't clear enough.

Whatever Willow had expected him to tell her, it wasn't that. Her mouth hung open slightly as she tried to take it in. That didn't altogether sound like their land was safe after all.

'But what about Andrew?'

182

A cloud crossed Jude's face for an instant. 'I'll tell you about that later.' Willow was about to ask a further question, when Jude jumped in again. 'And I know that probably sounds like the most horrendous news you've ever heard, but you're not to worry. Financially, the deal was a very good one, so we're not going to be penniless for a good while yet; besides it's more a matter of what I want to do with the rest of my life, or more importantly what *we* want to do with the rest of our lives.'

Willow's letter was growing hot in her hand. 'And what do you want to do with the rest of your life?' she asked cautiously.

Jude plucked the letter out of her grasp and took both her hands in his. He raised them to his mouth and gently kissed each one in turn.

'I want to spend some more time with my gorgeous wife, and find out just how incredible her talents are. I want to watch our girls growing up instead of blinking and waving them off to university as virtual strangers, and I want never to have to wear a tie again . . . well, not often anyway.' He grinned. 'But most importantly, I want to nurture our family and the land around us. Other people can buy and sell property and land for huge sums of money, but I'm not going to be one of them, not any more.'

Willow watched Jude as he spoke, a mixture of emotions playing across his face. Mostly excitement, but now also a little nervous, as if unsure how his momentous decision would be received.

'Well, I'm not sure that I want you around all day, under my feet, getting in the way, making a mess . . . '

She winked at his astonished face.

'. . . Actually, I can't think of anything nicer,' she admitted. 'To be honest, I wish you'd done it years ago – all this striving for an even bigger pot of money that we didn't need, when pretty much everything we could wish for is right here . . . ' She gave a twinkly smile. 'And anything else is on next-day delivery from Amazon.'

Jude visibly relaxed. 'You really don't

mind then? I know I should have talked things over with you before, but there was so much to go wrong, and even up until the last minute, I wasn't sure it would all go through. I didn't want us to start to believe in the kind of life we could make for ourselves and then have it all torn away from us if things didn't work out. I didn't think I could bear that for you.' He rubbed a thumb over the back of her hand. 'Although . . . by some weird stroke of fate, I think you might be one step ahead of me anyway . . . or have I got that wrong?'

Willow blushed, a sheepish smile on her face. 'I'm guilty of keeping things to myself too,' she said. 'I've been exploring some new ways of expanding the business here, things that complement the fruit farm. I kind of hoped that if I got it off the ground, I'd have a viable idea to put to you . . . and now might be the perfect time to tell you what I've been up to, especially as this arrived in the post this morning.'

She handed Jude the letter with a

slightly shaking hand, not yet having had a chance to fully absorb its contents herself. She waited anxiously while he read it, wondering what he was thinking. It had been so wrong not to share any of what she had been up to the past few weeks, she knew that now, but at the time it had seemed right; a decision which now seemed silly and misguided.

Jude's raised voice broke into her thoughts.

'Bloody hell!' He grinned. 'I've been reading about these places in one of the business magazines I subscribe to. The bloke that owns them is an organic farmer and he started with just one small guesthouse at his own place, which his wife ran, but now they have eight, very select and very exclusive small hotels, which are currently on the lips of every famous blogger and YouTuber around.'

'I know!' Willow grinned back. 'I've been experimenting with a range of ice creams and cordials, and to cut a long story short, Merry has been sending out some sample packs to people she has contacts with.'

'And they want to talk to you about supplying all their hotels, not just the kitchen but the guest rooms too . . . Willow, this is amazing!' he burst out, excitement mounting once more. 'I said you were a woman of spectacular talents.' He paused for a moment. 'I don't suppose,' he started, more seriously, 'that you might need a little help from a chap who's pretty good at marketing, and making the tea and whatever else you need, and who has suddenly become comprehensively unemployed?'

Willow beamed the smile she had been waiting a long time to deliver. 'I don't think there's anything I'd like more,' she said, holding Jude's look. 'I've no idea how all this is going to pan out, or how busy we might get, but I'd much rather be doing it with you by my side.'

She took a breath, wondering how best to frame her next question. 'This might sound a bit weird, even for me,' she began. 'But I've had some . . . dreams lately, they only started a few weeks ago, but last night I woke from a particularly vivid one, only to realise that they might not have been my dreams after all . . . but someone else's.'

Jude shifted uncomfortably in his chair. 'Go on,' he said.

'And don't ask me how, but it's almost as if I was picking up on your thoughts . . . although I'm not sure thoughts is quite the right word. They were a bit stronger than that.'

'What kind of thoughts?'

Willow pulled at the end of her plait. 'Maybe I had better just come out with it. You'll either laugh, or . . . ' She sat up a little straighter. 'I've seen images of the land up beyond Henry's house, at some point in the future I'm guessing. Only not as it is now, but torn up, built on, a mass of houses and roads and I —'

Jude visibly paled, swallowing hard. 'How could you possibly know that?' he whispered. 'How could you know what I've seen . . . what frightened me more than anything in this whole business?'

Willow clutched at his hand. 'It terrified me too, to see the meadows all gone, everything destroyed.'

'It'll never happen, Willow, you have my promise. I've seen to it that Andrew never —'

'Andrew?' echoed Willow, confused. With all that had happened over the past couple of days, she had forgotten her original belief that Andrew was behind the sale of their land, but now Jude had sold his share of the business, it didn't make any sense. Her thoughts were churning.

'But what about Andrew's share in the business? And you've done some sort of a deal with Henry, I know you have. I saw you both outside the bank yesterday, shaking hands. What was that all about?'

Jude gave a wry smile. 'Ah, Henry . . . ' he said. 'Yes, that was . . . unexpected. But listen, let me tell you about Andrew first. As you can imagine, he wasn't over the moon when I told him I wanted out of the business, but in the end he really had no choice.' He cleared his throat before continuing. 'You'll remember the night a few weeks back when I came home really late, and in a bit of a state to put it mildly. I made out I'd been led astray by some Japanese businessman, when actually what happened was that I presented my father with the details of the sale I'd already negotiated. After a . . . heated discussion . . . we agreed that from here on in, I was no longer fit to call myself his son.'

Willow's hand flew to her throat as her eyes filled with tears. 'Oh Jude, why didn't you tell me?' she said, anger flaring. 'How could he do such a thing?'

'Because he's an unfeeling sanctimonious bastard I suspect. He's never loved me, Willow, I know that now. I've spent my life trying to please him, to make him take notice of what I achieved in the hope that he might deign to throw me a crumb of affection, but it's never going to happen. Now I've woken up to the fact, I'm rather surprised to find that I'm looking forward to taking my own decisions and living my own life without his influence.' He smiled at Willow again. 'Despite what he thinks, I happen to believe that I've made some very sound choices in my life so far.'

Willow searched Jude's face as he regarded her calmly and with more than a little affection. He was telling the truth, and it must have taken a lot of guts to face up to it, let alone come to terms with it. Willow couldn't pretend to be anything other than overjoyed to have Andrew out of their lives for good, even though its legacy must be hard for Jude.

'I know he's never liked me, but —' She stopped suddenly as she realised what Jude's words would actually mean for them. 'But what about the house, and the land? My strawberries! Oh, God, Jude, we'll have to leave and . . . ' She couldn't bear the thought of it, not now, not when she had come so close to making things happen.

Jude took hold of her hands again and chuckled. 'No, we won't, and believe me that's absolutely the best bit. Wonderfully ironic too; it was your strawberries that were his downfall in the end.'

Willow gave him a quizzical look.

'There've been many occasions over the years when Andrew has suggested selling the meadows, but this time he'd even gone so far as to suss out the potential for getting planning permission, and snaring a buyer who was happy to do a deal on a speculative purchase. No doubt, had the sale gone ahead, Andrew would have done everything in his power to make sure planning was granted and the resultant kick back from any houses built would have netted a small fortune. There was only one problem with the proposed sale – well two actually.'

'And they were?'

'Well, first, that I was dead set against it, but second, and more importantly, that to build any houses on the land, you'd need to have an access route . . . and the only two possible routes would be through our strawberry fields or up the lane behind Henry's house. Of course the best one would be through our fields, or rather, as Andrew put it, "through that silly little business of your wife's". He even asked me to have a chat with you and talk you out of running it.' Jude held up his hand as he caught the expression on Willow's face.

'In the end, that was what made me stop and think. Apart from the brazen cheek of it, he made me realise how important our fields are and that in fact we have a proper future here together which is worth more to me than anything I could ever earn. It made me even more determined not to sell the land.'

Willow nodded. 'So you needed to find a way to get Andrew out of the business ...'

'... No, the other way around. I needed to find a way to get me out of it, and everything we have here along with me.'

'But how did you do that?'

'It was quite simple in the end. I just played to his love of money. Andrew can't run the business, he doesn't have the skill, and he never has had. So despite what he thought of me, he needed me plain and simple ... or someone else who could take my place, keep the company afloat, and keep Andrew's investment paying out at a nice steady rate. Without that someone else, the company would fold, and bang would go Andrew's income. Middleton Estates is currently holding two huge parcels of land that I acquired some years ago. Bought speculatively, but shrewdly, and which have now fallen into areas ripe for development. In fact, one has already had planning permission granted on it. If we simply sold the company outright, Andrew would get his payout, admittedly, but by staying in the game, he stands to net a huge fortune from the building of the houses too. So it wasn't much of a choice after all. I've sold my share in the company to a third party, and Andrew gets to keep his millions. He might be a materialistic bastard, but he's not stupid.'

Willow gazed at her husband, trying to take in everything he had told her.

'But you've given up all that money too . . .' she said.

'Yep,' grinned Jude. 'I decided it wasn't

worth as much as I thought it was.' He kissed her nose. 'And besides, I'm not that magnanimous. I made sure I got exactly what I wanted.'

'Which was?'

'A certain sum of money —' he winked '— but more importantly, my price included this house, the strawberry fields, all the meadows, the office . . . '

'Henry's house?'

'Yes, that too. It all belongs to us now.'

'You really have worked all this out, haven't you?'

Jude picked her letter up from the table and waved it at her. 'As have you if I'm not very much mistaken.' He read the letter through again. 'I even love the name Willowberries – it's just perfect!'

'Do you really? It seemed right some-how, but I probably wasn't thinking properly at the time. I mean, we should have something that reflects both of us, shouldn't we?'

Jude leaned forward and kissed Willow squarely before she could say any more. 'No, I like it just the way it is,' he said, eyes shining. 'And our buyers are going to love it!'

Willow returned his kiss, her stomach fizzing with excitement at the prospect of what was to come. She was about to show him some of the things she had been up to when she remembered what she had to say to Jude. On the face of it everything seemed perfect, but there was still the possibility that things could come crashing down around her ears. She looked up into Jude's clear blue eyes.

'I have an apology to make,' she said. 'I've been going out of my mind these last few weeks, what with these dreams, and fears about what was going to happen. Everything has been so confusing, I almost didn't know what to believe . . . but I should have talked to you about it. I should have told you my ideas for this place, asked for your help and support instead of arrogantly going ahead with what I believed was right. I feel like I haven't trusted you, like I've let you down . . . ' Her eyes filled with tears.

Jude touched her cheek, his eyes shining with emotion too. 'No, I should have told you . . . shared all of this with you before, but I was so scared I couldn't make it happen. I wouldn't have been able to bear it for you if we started to believe in what our lives could be like and then have it all taken away from us. It would have been the cruellest blow, and I thought it better if you didn't know.'

'Promise me that whatever happens in the future we will never keep secrets from each other again?'

Jude nodded gently. 'I promise . . . although there is just one other tiny thing I ought to tell you,' he added quietly, 'but it's a good thing, I swear!'

'Is this about Henry?' urged Willow. 'Please tell me it is. I still haven't figured out where he comes into this.'

'Well, no one was more surprised than me, but a couple of weeks ago, Henry came to see me offering to buy his house. Outright, in cash for a quick sale. I really had no idea, but he's completely minted . . . Anyway, I had to tell him what I was planning, but I swore him to secrecy. I didn't even know myself at the time if it would be possible, but the more I thought about his offer, the more it made sound sense, for all of us. Yesterday, once I knew the deal was going through, I was able to firm things up with him. That's when you saw us in town I guess.'

Willow blushed slightly remembering her wild thoughts of the day before. 'Well, that does explain that,' she said. 'Although he's never mentioned anything about buying the house before . . . ' Her eyes suddenly widened. 'Hey, I wonder if this has anything to do with Delilah?'

'Well, he's asked to rent the first meadow from us as well.'

'Really? Whatever does he want that for?'

Jude smiled slowly. 'To keep goats on of course. Or, more accurately, for Delilah to keep goats on. I rather think they've fallen in love.'

'Oh, of course!' exclaimed Willow, and

suddenly everything in her world fell into the most magical and perfect place.

14

It was the end of a very hot and very busy week, but sprawled in the meadow under the big oak tree, Willow had never been happier. Excited chatter and burbles of laughter reached her as she looked around at her group of friends enjoying a long cool drink in the evening sun. A slight breeze rustled the tall heads of the grasses that fringed the field and tickled their skin as they walked by, each of them revelling in the knowledge that, albeit for different reasons, life was about to get a lot more interesting.

As a result of the article in *Country Living*, Merry now had more customers than she knew what to do with, but she was taking it all in her stride and looking forward to being able to make all the dreams she had for their shop come true a little quicker. And of course more customers for Merry, meant more people to buy Willowberries' ice creams and cordials; not that it looked as though they were going to need many more customers just at the moment, because plans for their cookery courses and working holidays were coming along nicely too . . .

Henry and Delilah had to be peeled apart from one another at regular intervals as they forged ahead with plans for their new life together, and Freya and Sam had plans too, having finally decided to set a date for their wedding — after the harvest had been safely gathered in of course. The honeymoon would have to wait a while, but they would be pressing the first of their fruit together as man and wife and that was the most important thing. It all had the most wonderful symmetry about it, thought Willow.

Even Peter, who was lying flat on his back staring up at the evening sky would be a part of everything. Her idea to ask him to play a greater role in the development of Willowberries had not been hers alone. Jude had also spotted his potential, and, with a bit of frank discussion, Peter had been delighted with the offer Jude had made him. It had taken a while to organise, but by switching his course, he could finish his degree part-time, commuting the now much shorter distance to uni on the days he needed to attend and, on the others, honing his business skills. So far, he was shaping up to be a very fine apprentice indeed.

Willow waved a nonchalant hand as a bee passed a little too close to her drink for comfort.

Merry giggled. 'See, it's so good, even the bees want it back,' she said, raising her own glass as if in a toast. 'May the bees always pollinate your flowers, Willow,' she added.

'I might have to start giving them a bit as a thank-you present,' she replied. 'Especially if we do decide to start making honey and ginger ice cream. Got to keep 'em sweet,' she said, laughing at her own joke. She looked at Merry's happy face for a moment, knowing that she was just as contented.

Beside her, Jude cleared his throat,

topping up her glass.

'I think it's time for a toast,' he said, raising his voice above the general hubbub. 'What do you all say?'

Sam pulled Freya from where she was lounging against him into a more upright position. 'I think that's a fine idea,' he agreed. 'Come on, Freya, what shall we drink to?'

'Only one thing we can drink to, I reckon.' She giggled. 'To all of us, to the future!' she cried.

'To the future!' they chorused.

Willow looked at her husband over the rim of her glass. His skin was golden from days spent outside, his lithe body relaxed, and his beautiful face so often turned towards her that she found herself blushing. Far from causing a rift between them the events of the last few months had brought them closer together than ever. To have him by her side day by day was more than she could ever have wished for.

★ ★ ★

Jude took a sip of his drink as he watched his two daughters playing a little distance away. He took Willow's hand as he looked out across the fields and watched the sun sink lower in the sky, feeling nothing but relief at the knowledge that he had been saved.

Jude Middleton was a very lucky man. He may have been afraid of being poor once upon a time, and he may have been afraid of not being loved, but for the first time in his life, Jude Middleton was no longer afraid, of anything.